A FAIRY TALE

'Solly, you remember Eunice Goldberg's daughter Linda that we all thought was such an ugly duckling? Well, look what a swan she's turned into. And not married, either!' She treated me to one of her most suggestive winks, thrust the unsuspecting Linda Goldberg upon me, and disappeared into the crowd, her antennae quivering as she searched out new victims for her matchmaking magic.

Linda Goldberg, it turns out, is not all bad. She is only a couple of years younger than I am, and it seems that she has been getting the same thing from her mother that I have been getting from my aunt. Now she stares at me balefully through her glasses.

'I'm ugly,' she says. 'What's your excuse?'

'Even worse,' I whisper. 'I'm gay.'

A FAIRY TALE

a
novel
by

S. STEINBERG

Star

A STAR BOOK

published by
the Paperback Division of
W. H. ALLEN & Co. Ltd

A Star Book
Published in 1981
by the Paperback Division of
W. H. Allen & Co. Ltd
A Howard and Wyndham Company
44 Hill Street, London W1X 8LB

First published in Great Britain by
W. H. Allen & Co. Ltd, 1980

Printed in Great Britain by
Hunt Barnard Printing, Aylesbury, Bucks.

ISBN 0 352 30973 3

This book is for so many people—
Emily and Yvonne, who always
gave lots of love and friendship;
Jane, who believed in the book and
in me; and, of course, David and
Paul, who never got upset when
"Maudie" pounded on the
typewriter all night.

—S. STEINBERG

1

"Solly Steinberg, have I got a girl for you!"

The words bounced off the ceiling, skittered against the far wall, and, even though I did my best to duck, hit me with the full force that only an aunt under a full head of steam can muster. The champagne glass in my hand bent, but quickly recovered itself (the elegance of cut crystal executed in plastic), and I raised my voice, cackling loudly at one of my Uncle Marvin's tasteful jokes about traveling salesmen. Not, of course, that it did me any good at all. Aunt Sylvia bore down on me, dragging behind her a hapless piece of wreckage in a shapeless beige silk dress (no doubt a discount-store copy of an Ohrbach's replication of a once-respectable original), peering vacantly through harlequin-framed glasses, her face surrounded by a rather unfortunate version of a "natural." Aunt Sylvia, however, wore a smile of pure euphoria.

"Solly, you remember Eunice Goldberg's daughter Linda that we all thought was such an ugly duckling? Well, look what a swan she's turned into. And not married, either!" She treated me to one of her most suggestive winks, thrust the unsuspecting Linda Goldberg upon me, and disappeared into the crowd, her antennae quivering as she searched out new victims for her matchmaking magic.

I shouldn't have been surprised, really. Every time I turn up for the latest in what is apparently to be an unending series of family weddings, the same thing happens. Aunt Sylvia dispatches Uncle Hymie to the airport while she waits at home on Roxbury Drive (south of Sunset, but you can't have everything) working up a good cry. By the time Uncle Hymie has dragged me back to Beverly Hills, Aunt Sylvia is ready. She opens the door, wipes away a tear, blows her nose, and says, "Solly, this year I was hoping it would be you. You're not getting any younger, you know. I hope you ate on the plane—I didn't cook." Then, the first dose of guilt expertly administered, she lovingly pulls me into the kitchen, where the food she didn't cook—a meat loaf, two chickens, some gefilte fish, a leftover brisket, plus noshes—is laid out on the table. I get the immediate feeling that I am being fattened up as an offering to the virgins. By Aunt Sylvia's definition, a virgin is any unmarried Jewish girl under thirty (the limit rises to thirty-five in three more years) who has no debilitating deformities. (Until last year, a club-foot was considered a disqualifying deformity, but on my thirty-second birthday Aunt Sylvia lowered the standards, which led to a rather difficult evening at a disco.)

Once I have been fed, the campaign begins in earnest. Aunt Sylvia runs down the list of candidates from my previous visit, updating me on the lives of each of them, giving particular attention to those girls who have, since last I was in the area, married doctors or lawyers. Then she gets to the newest additions.

"Do you remember Annette Weisman?"

I do indeed remember Annette Weisman, but Aunt Sylvia assures me that her second nose job was much better than the first: "Still not quite right, mind you, but anything would have been an improvement, and Annette needs all the encouragement she can get. You'll take her to the rehearsal dinner."

You can imagine what it's like: each day, as the impending wedding looms ever closer, Aunt Sylvia becomes more frantic. By the time of the actual wedding, the bride and groom are shoved unceremoniously aside—*they*, after all, have fulfilled their duty by getting married, and will, no doubt, immediately set about the task of producing grandchildren—and Aunt Sylvia, feeling that I might be weakened by the joy of the event and the flowing of the champagne, has found herself a Linda Goldberg.

Linda Goldberg, it turns out, is not all bad. She is only a couple of years younger than I am, and it seems she has been getting the same thing from her mother that I have been getting from my aunt. Now she stares at me balefully through her glasses.

"I'm ugly," she says. "What's your excuse?"

"Even worse," I whisper. "I'm gay."

2

I spent the rest of the evening with Linda Goldberg, which was not so bad. We did our best to look like we were falling in love, and Aunt Sylvia and Linda's mother had the good grace to keep their distance. At midnight I flew back to San Francisco, rescued my twin poodles, Mitzie and Fritzie, from their Aunt Scott, and went home. Something, I decided, had to be done. The time was coming when I was going to have to tell Aunt Sylvia to stop shopping for a wife for me. On the other hand, I had been coming to this decision after every wedding for the last five years. This time, as usual, I did what I always do. Let a sleeping dog lie. I mean, how do you tell the aunt who raised you that all is not as she would like it to be? Write her a letter, maybe? I thought about doing that a few years ago. She had sent me a book for my birthday, about a fat, ugly Jewish girl (Linda Goldberg?) who was going to kill herself because she couldn't find a man (Linda Goldberg!). So I read the book, got the hint, and decided the time had come. I sat down, pen in hand, and began writing:

First, [I said] thank you for the birthday card. Not that I'm admitting to being thirty-one, [I'm still not] but if I hide the thing carefully, perhaps in the vegetable bin, maybe nobody will notice. I think twenty-eight is a much nicer age to be, and I have every intention of being twenty-eight for several more years. So you and I know the truth —do we have to talk about it?

Now, as to the book. I've read it, and I'm not impressed. All right, so the poor broad is my age and not married. What does she expect, being a fat, ugly, Jewish girl? She thinks maybe men grow on trees? Believe me, they don't. I may be Jewish, but I'm not fat, ugly, or a girl, and I know: *men do not grow on trees.* But am I going to kill myself over it? Am I going to stick my head in an oven? Am I going to slit my wrists? No, Aunt Sylvia, I'm not. I'm going to go right on doing what I've been doing. I'm going to pull myself together, put on a nice sweater, pretend it's still 1968, and go out and find a man.

At this point I stopped writing, because I could hear Aunt Sylvia's voice all the way from Beverly Hills: "A man? My nephew is going to go out and find himself a *man?* What have I raised? What kind of pervert did I nourish at my bosom?"

What do I say in response to that? "That's right,

Aunt Sylvia, you got yourself a queer nephew''? She'd be running off to make Uncle Hymie rip the buttons off his vest before I could point out she'd never nourished me at her bosom, let alone that things could be a lot worse: I could be a child molester. (Contrary to popular belief, very few faggots are child molesters. It simply isn't done, except in a few weird cases, and in those cases said molesters are ostracized. Us fairies can rip a pretty good button ourselves, when the occasion arises.)

You can see why I didn't bother to finish that letter, let alone put it in an envelope and mail it. Aunt Sylvia may not be the easiest person in the world to live with, but I don't live with her—not anymore—and if she got a letter like that one, she'd have dragged me home for some chicken soup before I could have even walked the dogs. So I stuck it away in my desk, and decided that there were some things Aunt Sylvia just didn't need to know. On the other hand, why shouldn't she know?

Maybe if I told her all about it. . . .

3

Let's get right back to where it all started, when I was eight years old and the kid down the block and I decided to play with each other's peepees. Don't snicker, please; that's what we called it. But it didn't work out too well. For one thing, every time we did it the little peepees got hard, and obviously that wasn't what was supposed to happen. That's what we thought, anyway. Ha! Little did *we* know! So we gave it up after a few tries. If that was sex, who needed it? A few years later I found out that that *wasn't* sex, and that *I* needed it.

Skipping ahead a few years, and leaving out all the pious baloney about "sensitive little boys," there was a kid named Morrie Goldberg. Come to think of it, Morrie was Linda's older brother, which may be a clue as to why she wasn't so upset when I told her I was gay. Anyway, Morrie had a lot of charm—he once shoved a firecracker up Aunt Sylvia's cat's ass, which did not endear him to Aunt Sylvia. I'm sure she hasn't forgotten him.

I haven't forgotten Morrie Goldberg, either

He had pubic hair at the age of twelve.

He's the one who told me it was *supposed* to get hard, and showed me what happened when it did. Oh boy, did he show me!

That was the day I found out about sodomy.

Maybe Aunt Sylvia *should* have known. I mean, even though nobody talked about such things back then, I suppose I *was* one of those "sensitive" little boys. If I wasn't, why did everyone say I was? But let's be honest.

I wasn't sensitive, I was nelly.

Sensitive little boys don't go out on Halloween. They stay home and hope nothing will go bump in the night. Nelly little boys haul out their sister's clothes, get in drag, slap on a yarn wig, and go out to terrorize the neighborhood. No, I was definitely not "sensitive." And about that yarn wig—granted, nobody had invented Dynel yet, but those yarn ringlets didn't do a thing for my big brown eyes, and wool simply will *not* hold a set in a good fog.

And while we're on the subject of my youth, which frankly wasn't all that hot a period of my life, we might as well talk a little bit about the great American pastime, self-abuse. Only we didn't call it self-abuse. We called it jacking off, pounding off, beating off, pulling your pud (*I* never called it that, but some people did), or, if we wanted to be technical, masturbation. Only we didn't spell it with a *u*. We spelled it with an *e*, thus making it very difficult to look up in *Van Nostrand's Scientific Encyclopedia* and find out the Real Truth. Had masturbation been spelled with an *e* instead of a *u*, I probably could have finally put to rest the great myth that jerking off (we called it *that*, too) causes you to grow hair on the palms of your hands. I, of course, knew there was no truth to the rumor. If there had been, my right thumb and forefinger would have been sporting mustaches at age thirteen, and I'd have had a full beard to the right wrist in the eighth grade. Wouldn't that have caused talk? Little Solly Steinberg, who has to shave his hand before school every morning. Also, sometimes in the afternoon or before dinner.

So anyway, I finally figured out how to spell "masturbation," and I looked it up. Not a word about hairy hands. There was some drivel about it being psychologically habit-forming, but I was so hooked I didn't pay any attention to that. All I knew was that it felt good.

But to return to the subject of my youth and the immortal question: Should Aunt Sylvia have known? Come to think of it, why should she have? I barely knew myself. In my golden youth, which in my crowd is referred to as that dismal time when we thought we were the only one, the guys I was doing it with were only "messing around." *They* weren't queer. (Bet *me* they weren't queer. I remember the handsome stud in high school—the one all the girls were going wild over, that everyone said would have to get married. He's married all right: to an ex-marine and they run a poodle parlor in Seattle!) So if we didn't know, why should Aunt Sylvia have known?

On the other hand, now I know, and what do I have? I have Aunt Sylvia beating her breast because I'm not married. I mean, it isn't like I'm another Linda Goldberg. What she has could be fixed; whose fault is it that her family wouldn't admit that their swan was a duck, and a pretty ugly one at that? A little honesty, a good diet, and some surgery, and they could all be smashing wineglasses instead of hanging crepe. And as for Linda, she made some mumblings about how a dyke once had the hots for her. So what's the big deal? She wanted a husband—I ask you: what's better, a husband with tits, or no husband at all? Forget I asked. Linda told me the dyke got married, leaving Linda with nothing but her memories and pimple cream.

But what could have been done for me?

Surgery?

I have a perfectly good nose.

A diet?

Fat is not my main concern.

My main concern, as it happens, is not all that much different from Aunt Sylvia's: here I am, on the slimy side of thirty, and single. Not, of course, that I have always been single. No, indeed. So I guess you might say my chances of finding a man are a little better than Linda's. I mean, I've done it before, so I should be able to do it again.

So there I sat, in the dead of night, having survived one more of Aunt Sylvia's frontal attacks on what she thinks is my bachelorhood. I am not as young as I used to be, and I am getting tired. It is time, I decided, to take the bull by the horns and tell Aunt Sylvia the Real Truth. So I sent her a telegram:

DEAR AUNT SYLVIA—HAVE DECIDED I AGREE WITH YOU, AND WOULD LIKE TO GET MARRIED. DO YOU KNOW ANY NICE JEWISH BOYS? BEST REGARDS, SOLLY.

The telegram on its way, I went to bed.

It is amazing how fast mail can get to you sometimes.
I sent that telegram on a Saturday night. By Monday
there was a letter in my mailbox. If you could call it a
letter. It was from Aunt Sylvia, and I got the distinct
impression she was upset about something. What she
said, and I will quote it, is as follows:

Dear Solomon, [Already I know I am in trouble.]

My life is over. How will I ever be able to hold
my head up again? I haven't told Hymie anything.
It would kill him. That such a thing could happen
in our family! How could you do such a thing to
me? And don't you have any feeling for your
Uncle? For shame, Solomon! For shame!

She signed it "Love, Aunt Sylvia," which I suppose
was more by reflex action than anything else.

Well, I thought, thanks a lot for the dose of shame. I only hope antibiotics work as well on shame as they do on clap. Also, do I have to stop drinking till the shame goes away?

What did I do to her? And to Uncle Hymie? Uncle Hymie, at whom I've never even made so much as a slight pass? It made me feel like I'd brought leprosy into the house. Maybe I should send back the shame, and ask her to send me a bell. Instead I decided to try a diversionary tactic. I dropped her a very nice note that afternoon, mentioning that since she was now calling me Solomon (which I detest), instead of Solly (which always had a sort of friendly ring to it), she might as well know that *nobody* calls me Solly anymore. I changed my name to Murray Roberts years ago. I mean, who ever heard of a decorator named Solly Steinberg?

The diversion only made things worse!

Dear Solly, [she wrote.] [On the other hand, maybe things are getting better after all!] Murry Roberts? What kind of name is Murry Roberts? [Things are not getting better. Now I am in a new kind of trouble.] Have you been dating a shiksa? If you have, don't bring her home. It would be worse for Uncle Hymie than knowing you're queer, may he never find that out, either. I've been thinking it over. You remember that boy you brought home from college that time? The acting student named Bruce? Was he queer too? He seemed so nice.

She signed it "Love," but I wasn't so sure. I mean, how much love can she feel for me, when she's convinced I'm trying to kill Uncle Hymie? I stared at the letter for a long time, wondering whether it was worth my while to point out that there is an *a* in Murray. Also, I wondered if it would be possible to convey to her that the term these days is "gay," not "queer." Queer implies something strange, and it's not strange to be gay anymore. It's getting so it's strange not to be. Queer is what you are before you find out you're gay. And as for Bruce, what was her first clue? Perhaps the fact that the extra bed in my room was not slept in? What has she been thinking all these years, that Bruce slept on the floor?

Perhaps, since Aunt Sylvia brought up the subject of college, I should mention a couple of things about those wonderful formative years. After my golden youth (mentioned earlier) I decided the best thing to do was get out of Beverly Hills while the getting was good. So I went to the Midwest, which you'll have to admit is not Beverly Hills. Being a nice Jewish boy, I chose a nice liberal school where they were willing to talk about anything. One of the things they talked about was homosexuality, and what they said was that they didn't have any. (Apparently they equated it with good food—they didn't have any of that, either.) Well, it turns out there *was* homosexuality there. The frustrated kind. Being, myself, terribly naive, I didn't even realize when passes were being made at me. When I think back now, some of the boys I could have had . . . What the hell, no sense crying over spilled milk, is there?

Anyway, when I found out there was no homosexuality in the Midwest (on the theory that if it wasn't at that nice liberal college, it wasn't anywhere in the area), I decided to try my fortunes elsewhere and went to Montana. (I must have been having a butch attack that year.) It was in Montana that I found out that college students do it too. Until then I had assumed that messing around with boys was something you gave up along with high school.

What happened was, there was a party. Oh, boy, was there a party! Somehow, and don't ask me how, I wound up in a Murphy bed with an anthropology major whose name I never did find out, and a graduate in drama (what else?) named François Fromage. (Do you believe François Fromage? I don't either. I wonder what it was before he changed it.) Anyway, there the three of us were, little Solly Steinberg in the middle, and all of a sudden I notice that there is a hand stroking my left thigh. Then I notice that there is another hand stroking my right thigh. Not one to object to a good thing, I don't move. Pretty soon there are two hands aimed toward my crotch. Well, I'm not exactly a princess teeny-meat, but on the other hand, there's only so much room in one crotch, right? So what happens? The two hands meet at the designated spot, and start holding each other. Meanwhile, Solly, the object of both men's attention, is left out in the cold and getting very, very horny.

So I groped them both.

Naturally they returned the favor, and the moment of truth came when both the hands on my crotch tried to grab at the same time. There was a sort of quick clutch and instant withdrawal. Like they both dropped out of the race. Being the man in the middle, I made my choice and suggested to François Fromage that we adjourn to my apartment, which happened to be conveniently located only a block away, and was conveniently empty that weekend, since my roommate, an anal-compulsive number, had finished washing the light bulbs early and gone off to visit his family in the eastern wilderness.

So off we went, crawled into bed, played with each other till the sheets were messy, then went off to sleep.

Next sound heard is a door opening, and next sight seen is dear old roommate peering into the bedroom. First he sees that I am not alone. This does not shock him. (Even anal compulsives have a certain degree of sophistication.) Then he sees that I am in bed with a man. This shocks him. Then he sees that the man is François Fromage.

"Mr. Fromage," he says, eyes popping out. "What are you doing here?"

"Oh, shit," says Fromage. "Make the world go away."

How was I to know I'd balled one of my roommate's former high school teachers? I stuck around just long enough for the frost to hit the air, then struck out for home. And when I got home, I found out a few things:

1. I was not queer. I was gay.
2. The world is full of people like me. . . .
3. Even married men.
4. If you're young, pretty, and gay, living at home with Aunt Sylvia and Uncle Hymie is not where it's at.

5

What, you are asking, is the difference between queer and gay? Don't deny it—I can hear you. "What is with Solly," you're saying? "What is with queer and gay? Queer *is* gay. I know—I looked it up." Of course that's what you're saying. Well, don't forget, I looked up "masturbation" (once I found out about the *u*) and it didn't tell me a damned thing.

Experience! That's what you need. The great teacher! That's how I found out the difference between queer and gay. So now, out of my great wisdom, I shall enlighten you.

Queer is what you are before you find out you're not the only one in the world. Gay is what you become when you find out you are not alone. Let's face it—wouldn't you tend to get a little giggly yourself if you suddenly found out you weren't the only person in the whole world?

Queer is what heterosexual perverts call you. Perverts, you ask? You're linking "heterosexual" and "pervert"? What kind of sick person are you, you're asking. Face it—if you think what I do is weird (and you don't know the half of it yet), what do you think *I* think of what you do? Are you following me? Remember, perversion is in the eye of the nonindulger. People keep telling me you are what you eat. Incorrect. You are *who* you eat. So let's get down to specifics:

Queer is what you are when the landlady isn't going to rent you the apartment.

Gay is what you are when she's going to cut the rent so you'll move in.

Queer is what you are when your boss fires you.

Gay is what you are when you sue him for it.

Queer is what you were in Tularosa, New Mexico.

Gay is what you are in San Francisco.

Are you beginning to get the idea? So now that you're getting the idea, let's get on to Point Two: The world is full of people like me.

Once upon a time I was working in a dumb job in East Los Angeles (one of the places that falls into the Tularosa, New Mexico, category, rather than San Francisco). There I was, being trained for an exciting career in which I would be paid five hundred a month to be sure that Floors Forever wasn't getting screwed out of three hundred a month in overcharges for shipping a bunch of ugly asphalt tile around the country. So I'm looking around one day, and what do I see? I see a gorgeous hunk of man looking at me. Not wanting to appear obvious, I turn to one of the secretaries and say, very coolly:

"Who's the queer over there on the order desk?"

Well, that garnered me a cold look, let me tell you. The broad was probably horny for him herself. So she looks at me, the corners of her mouth turned down, spits a little acid in my direction, and says:

"That's no queer. That's Harry, and he's married and has five children."

So what happens? Harry, who's married and has five children and isn't queer, gropes me in the men's room that afternoon. I begin to figure things out.

One thing leads to another, and Harry (who's married and has five children) wants to get together for drinks some night. So I'm not twenty-one, right? You think that matters? Hah! Drinks is not what Harry wants to get together with me for at all. What he really wants to get together with me for, is that the wife and five children don't do it for Harry, but I might. So who's objecting? Harry, from what I've seen in the men's room, might do it for me, too.

So Solly and Harry get together one night, find an abandoned house somewhere in the area (complete with beat-up mattress, lots of empty beer cans, and a stray rubber or two), and make the scene. I will admit that perhaps a motel room would have been more comfortable, but we did our best, kicking at empty beer cans, trying to avoid broken glass, and hoping that the wind wasn't going to freeze our tails off. Then we got to talking. A typical conversation between a twenty-year-old queer, and a thirty-two-year-old man of the world:

"How long have you been queer?" (That's the twenty-year-old queer talking, in case you hadn't guessed.)

"How long have I been what?"

"Isn't 'queer' the right word?"

"Well, that depends. Do you think you're queer?"

"I like men."

"So do I. So that makes me gay, not queer."

Being no dummy (whatever I am, you'll admit I'm no dummy), I figured that there was very little percentage in looking up "gay" in Funk and Wagnalls.

Now, yes. Then, forget it.

But I got the message. Suddenly the light dawned. I wasn't queer. I was gay. GAY! (Sounds of trumpets, and maybe a little fireworks.)

So Harry with a wife and five children (see Point Three, previous chapter: Even Married Men) let me in on a little secret: *There are lots of gay people in the world,* and there are places where they go to meet each other and not feel like queers.

These places, Harry tells me, are Gay Bars.

Not only that, but he actually been to some of them, and knows where they are. And so I discovered that there is a-whole-nother world. What did I do? I noted down the name of one of those things called Gay Bars, and formulated Rule One. Rule One goes as follows: Never get involved with a married man. (Harry I liked, but do I need a wife and five kids?) And I didn't, not for a long time. So, whatever Solly is, he's not a homewrecker. (I must remember to tell Aunt Sylvia that. That should make her throw another matzoh in the soup.)

Did I run off to a Gay Bar the next night? I did not. Not me. Not little Solly Steinberg. Oh, no. I was a lot cleverer than that. I'd read books. I'd heard stories. I knew what kind of people were likely to be in a Gay Bar. A lot of weird people who would attack you, tear off your pants, and molest you in the men's room, that's what kind of people hang out in Gay Bars. Was I going to let that happen to me?

I was clever, as I may have mentioned. I waited until one night when I was out on the town with a friend of mine. A straight friend. And then, when it was getting late, and we were fairly well shnockered, I aimed the old car down Melrose Avenue, got to La Brea, and said:

"Hey, there's the Red Raven."

"What's the Red Raven?" asked straight friend, falling right into things.

"It's a queer bar," I said, cool as you please. "Ever been in one?"

Straight out of Nebraska, he should ever have been in a Gay Bar? I was straight out of Beverly Hills, and I never had.

"No," he said, giving me the approved answer.

"Neither have I," said I, chuckling to myself. "Let's see what it's like."

So in we went, and guess what? It wasn't full of perverts running around tearing people's pants off and molesting them in the men's room. It was a whole roomful of gorgeous young men. So what happened to little Solly?

Diarrhea, that's what happened to little Solly.

Such an attack of the trots as you wouldn't believe. There I am, clutching a whiskey sour in one hand, and a cigarette in the other, and both hands shaking, and what's happening? I have to go to the head, that's what's happening. And what's going to happen in the head? There's going to be a lot of perverts waiting to rape me, that's what's going to happen.

Well, it finally came down to a decision. Go to the men's room and get raped, or crap on the floor. I chose the men's room.

I know you're not going to believe this, but I didn't get raped. Really, I didn't.

Instead, I sat there, with the sweat pouring off my

brow, feeling like a fool. So I pulled myself together, decided that the whole thing was ridiculous, and stomped back into the bar. I chugged down my drink, ordered another one, and wham! Another attack.

Back to the men's room.

By now I'm getting nervous, right? What's Ken from Nebraska going to think, right? Solly keeps running off to the men's room. Is Solly hoping he'll get molested? No! Solly's wishing he had a cork in his drawers!

After the third drink and the third attack, I suggested that maybe we ought to leave. Ken was having a good time watching the queers. I was not having a good time having diarrhea. We left.

All the way home, Ken kept talking about how everybody in there looked so normal. I didn't say anything. I was working on clenching my rectum.

A week later, I recovered. I decided to risk a return engagement on my own. I also decided that the whiskey sours had caused the diarrhea. I changed to Scotch and water.

Did you know that Scotch and water can cause diarrhea?

The second trip, I began to get into the swing of things. Everyone seemed to be talking to friends.

(What's this? Queers have friends? Another revelation!)

A few people, however, seemed to be as left out as I was. They were standing against the wall, a foot casually wrecking the paint job behind them, with their drinks jammed subtly into their shoulders (New York style). So I backed up to the wall, stuck my foot into the fireplace, and dropped my glass. Recovering, I changed positions in the room, got a new drink, and surveyed the situation. Finally I turned to the guy standing next to me, smiled brightly, and said:

"Are you just watching, too?"

He looked at me, did not smile brightly, and moved across the room. Apparently he wasn't just watching. Apparently he was cruising, a subject I didn't know anything about. However, since he didn't seem to want to talk to me, and nobody else was exactly charging in my direction, I left. Where did I go? Hollywood Boulevard, naturally. And what happened on Hollywood Boulevard? I got picked up.

That's right, little Solly Steinberg got picked up on Hollywood Boulevard.

Another smash. There I was, idly peering into windows and wondering why nobody at the Red Raven had talked to me, when somebody talked to me.

"Nice pair of pants, isn't it?" a voice says.

"Hanh?" I say, never at a loss for words.

"I said, it's a nice pair of pants, isn't it?"

"Which one?" says good old swift Solly.

"That one," says the voice. A hand appears, pointing.

"Un-hunh," says Mr. Small Talk, and moves on.

The voice follows.

"You live around here?"

I give a highly revealing shake of the head.

"Want a cup of coffee?"

I brighten. Oh, boy, do I want a cup of coffee. With about two quarts of Kaopectate in it. I nod brightly.

"Do you have a car?" says the voice. (What'd he think? I hitchhiked from Beverly Hills?) So I make some mumblings about how my car is parked in the next block, and before you can say Bar Mitzvah, we're on the way up to his place for coffee. He lives in a furnished single on Yucca Street, which I find out later is par for the course for new young queens around town, and I find a place to park. We enter the furnished single. He puts on the water for the coffee. Only it turns out that coffee isn't what he wants. He wants my body. Does he get my body? Hell, no, he doesn't get my body. He gets to pour coffee for me between attacks of diarrhea. I'll bet he dined out on that story for a month. He got a lot of free dinners; what did I get? A parking ticket.

Hooray for Hollywood.

Well, I guess that more or less covers the first few points. Now let's get on to the last one: If you're young, pretty, and gay, living at home with Aunt Sylvia and Uncle Hymie is not where it's at.

It was beginning to look like I was going to spend the rest of my life pinching nickels for Floors Forever, and having weekly attacks of diarrhea in Hollywood. Not, you have to admit, something to look forward to. There had to be a solution. And what was that solution? Go back to school.

He who goes to school can go to school where he wants, right? Right. And where did I want to go? San Francisco, right? Right! The Paris of the West. Baghdad by the Bay. Besides, I'd heard there were lots of queers there. And you know what? I'd heard right.

So off I went, changing my major from anthropology to interior design, and opening up a whole new world of pleasures, perils, and traumas.

Needless to say, I did not tell Aunt Sylvia the real reason I moved to San Francisco. Not, that is, until I got that last letter from her, asking me about Bruce. At that point, I decided she might as well know. I'm not sure she wanted to. . . .

6

Dear Solly,

The things you are telling me, I do not want to know. I'm not sure exactly what you are trying to tell me. Who can read, with the tears of an aunt staining every page? What you have done to me I cannot tell you. I am repulsed. I am revolted. I am disgusted. I am sick. I may have to tell Uncle Hymie, and if I do, God should help you. (But don't count on Uncle Hymie.)

So, I told Uncle Hymie.

He said "So what?" So, did you enjoy San Francisco?

Love,
Aunt Sylvia

Enjoy San Francisco? What is she talking about? Did she ever look for an apartment in San Francisco? Forget I asked. She married Uncle Hymie, and moved from the Fairfax to Beverly Hills. Fifty blocks from an apartment in a Jewish ghetto to a house in a Jewish ghetto is not exactly what I would call a big move. But from the house in Beverly Hills to a basement apartment in San Francisco? That's a big move.

Aunt Sylvia thinks me being gay is a problem? She should spend a week in San Francisco apartment-hunting. You have your choice: a big ugly building on Page Street (cockroaches, yes; hot water, no) or catch-as-catch-can in the big city. So off I went, looking for something decent.

First, there is a basement in a building on Green Street, Russian Hill address (very chic), but no windows. Also, the refrigerator is in the bedroom, and the bathroom is in the kitchen, which happens to be in the living room. I did not take it.

Then there is the building with the elegant entrance on Bush Street. Would I lie? That's how they advertised it: "Furnished junior three; elegant entrance." Junior three means there is an alcove with a mattress off the living room. Elegant entrance means there is a prissy middle-aged man with bleached hair, tight pants, and three cats who has freaked out with smoked mirrors, plastic ivy, and plaster columns in the lobby. Also, if you are a student, there is a fringe benefit. He does not lower the rent, but he accosts you regularly in the laundry room. If that's your scene, great. For me, I skipped it. (Being picked up on Hollywood Boulevard is one thing. Having chronic diarrhea in your own home is entirely another.)

I settled for Aspen Avenue.

Aspen Avenue is now very "in." It's been declared a historical area, a tried-and-true method for obtaining federal funds to fix the plumbing. When I was there, it was not historical. I waded to the bathroom every morning.

It wasn't too bad, really, till I found out that the people who rented me the apartment didn't own the building. But by that time the people had gone to Sweden, and I was getting tired of having to mop the floor ten times a week. So I moved. To Guerrero Street.

Guerrero Street was great, except for the lack of electricity. Not that there wasn't any. It's just that you had to be resourceful to get to it. I mean, one electrical outlet for an entire apartment? And that one in the middle of the ceiling? And a Murphy bed in the bathroom? I should have taken the basement on Green Street.

At least on Guerrero Street I had a roommate, which made things cheap. (Half of $150.00 a month is cheap, you have to admit.) Aunt Sylvia never met Bill. If she worried about Bruce, Bill would have made her *plotz!* Bill was into theater of violence—let's hear it for whips and chains! (More about that later.) Bill was straight, or at least I thought so until one night when I was proving my masculinity with a grubby little poetess from someplace in the South. There we were, the three of us (we were very modern) more or less making it on one of the couches. Bill, apparently, was trying to prove *his* masculinity, too. So what happens? I'm busy copping feels of Jeanine's tits in the best sophomoric tradition, and I can feel Jeanine playing with my balls. Then I hear Jeanine's voice whispering sweet nothings in my ear. The sweet nothing goes like this:

"Sweet-haht, you gonna have to make up yoah mind!"

"Eh?" (That's me, making clever conversation.)

"Well, Ah don' know, honey, but do you like boys or girls?"

"What are you talking about?"

"Well, Ah'm not quite sure how to put this, but that's not mah hand in yoah pants!"

Now that's what you call an eye-opener. I mean, if it wasn't Jeanine's, and it wasn't mine, it had to be someone else's.

Bill's.

Hot damn, I've got my first gay roommate. Only he's not my type. A crucial moment. I sort things out, come to a conclusion. I pick Jeanine up, carry her to the other couch, and fuck her. Bill stomps out, not forgetting to snap the light on as he leaves.

So I've lost my cherry. I am now a card-carrying heterosexual, right? Don't get your hopes up: Jeanine was lousy.

Bill moved out.

I moved to Church Street, decided that now that I'd had a girl, boys were definitely better, and got down to business.

Not, mind you, that I'd been practicing what you could call celibacy. Not me. No way. I'd found out a thing or two.

Namely, that I'd heard right: San Francisco *is* full of queers. (Now it's called the Gay Community. Then it was called full of queers. Things have changed.)

But I'd come up in the world. No more tawdry scenes in abandoned houses in East Los Angeles.

Try a tawdry scene in an empty apartment on Nob Hill. No broken glass, but on the other hand, no mattress, either.

No empty beer bottles, but, on the other hand, no heat.

San Francisco is much colder than East Los Angeles.

Get laid—get pneumonia.

Maybe Jeanine wasn't so bad after all.

But things were not all bad. In fact, once I got myself onto Church Street, and was able to keep myself in fresh flowers from the funeral parlor across the street, everything went much better.

Also, I found out about the Rendezvous.

That was San Francisco's answer to the Red Raven, but better. For one thing, I never got diarrhea at the Rendezvous. I never got clap, either, for whatever it's worth.

What I did get was an education. I found out a lot of things once I moved to Church Street and found the Rendezvous. For one thing, did you know that men actually sleep together? (You shouldn't fall off your chair—it's true! It came as a shock to me, too, but I survived.) Not that I *indulged* in it, of course.

A grope in the dark was one thing.

Sleeping with a man was entirely another.

But back to Church Street. That was some building, that one on Church Street. They didn't care who you were, or what you were—if you could pay the rent, you could live there. You, and your no-good husband, and your five sniveling brats with no necks and proclivities to pee in the elevator. If there were puddles in the elevator, you could use the stairs. Except they weren't very well lit, and the kiddies liked to leave piles on them. The whole place was sort of an early experiment in open housing.

Anyway, I should have been happy, right? There I was, young, pretty, and gay, living by myself in San Francisco. So it was the slums; it was still San Francisco.

Was I happy? You better believe I was happy. I was having a ball, and don't let anyone tell you any different. I was finding out what the world has to offer someone who is young, pretty, and gay, and lives alone in San Francisco. A sex education, that's what life has to offer. I feel sorry for those kids who are getting their sex education in school. They should get it in the streets, the way I did. You don't learn all the fancy terms for all the fancy positions. Instead, you learn the positions. I could perform fellatio long before I could spell it, and besides, didn't everyone always say that action speaks louder than words?

All was going well, but then something happened. I got married.

All right, so I didn't tell Aunt Sylvia right away. As a matter of fact, I waited ten years, and brought her up to date not so long ago. I figured, if I'm going to tell her the Real Truth, I should also tell her I got married. For a reasonably bright boy, I'm not always too smart.

7

Dear Solly,

You got married? Why didn't you tell us before! Don't tell me—you married a shiksa. But even so, Solly, we would have been there. Naturally not until after your Uncle Hymie recovered from the attack he would have had, but we'd have been there. I'd have made my special chopped chicken liver. (Do they eat chicken liver at Christian weddings?) What is her name? Why haven't you ever told us? And why haven't we ever met her?

I'm glad you gave up the homosexual thing. I've been reading up on it, and those queers are sick. Solly, those boys do weird things.

Bring your wife home sometime. Even if she's Catholic we'll be nice to her. If it's a Friday, we'll serve gefilte fish.

Love,
Aunt Sylvia

Boy, did she get the wrong idea!

I did not marry a shiksa. I married a goy. But not really, because he was converted. Already, before I met him, he was converted. Who ever heard of a Jewish tenor from Tulsa? You're right: nobody.

His name was Larry.

I use the past tense because I have a buttonless vest myself, but that's getting ahead of the story.

Love is strange. It does funny things to you. It makes you behave irrationally. It does me, anyway. So what happened, you're dying to know?

Well, there was this boy. Or most of a boy, since he was only about four and a half feet tall. He was a chorus boy. (I used to have a thing for chorus boys. I'd keep a file on them: names, real names, dates, places. Then, when they became stars, I'd have the documentary evidence that I once fucked a star. Only none of them became stars. The only time I fucked a star, I thought he was a chorus boy, but by then I'd given up the file, so I can't prove it. Is this what memories are made of?)

Anyway, there was this chorus boy, and after running into each other backstage at every theater in town, and one or two gay bars, we decided to make the scene. You already know what making the scene entails (remember fancy terms for fancy positions?), so I won't go into the grim details, except to tell you that he was the First. Before I knew what had happened, it had happened, if you know what I mean. So I went to the bathroom, threw up, and made out a file card with a red asterisk on it.

Then he introduced me to his lover. His lover, if I may say so, was not thrilled to meet the boy who'd been romping with his mate. I, on the other hand, was not thrilled to meet the lover. So we did what any self-respecting queens do in a situation such as that: we had a bitch-fight. And so I met Larry. Does it all sound like a cheap novel? I have news for you: my life *is* a cheap novel; maybe I can sell the movie rights, and Linda Lovelace can play me.

The bitch-fight was on Halloween.

I met Larry.

Larry met me.

We hated each other.

A good beginning.

Election night comes, and my phone rings.

"Is this Murray?" (That was the other voice, the one on the phone. By then it had become obvious to me that Solly Steinberg was not a name that was going to light up the world, except for perhaps Beverly Hills, which I was not about to go back to, so I changed it. So when the voice wanted to know if this was Murray, I knew right away they had the right number. Oh, boy, did they have the right number.)

"Just a minute. California's just coming in." That was me. If I die on election night, it better not happen till after California comes in.

There is a pause in the conversation, while IBM brings us California, which takes about three seconds from first precinct to final projection. Thank you, IBM, for finding a way to put the country to sleep early on election night. California is now in. So is Nixon. If I'd been smart, I'd have shot myself rather than live with Nixon, and that phone call would have never taken place.

"My life is over," I said. "Who's this?"

"Larry."

"I don't know anybody named Larry." The hell I didn't.

"You met me Halloween."

"I met lots of people Halloween. Were you wearing pants, or a dress?"

"I was Andy's lover."

"Why the use of the past tense?"

"I'm not Andy's lover anymore."

"Pity. It was a good match. He has a small body, and you have a small mind."

"Are you always vicious?"

"No. Sometimes I have laryngitis."

"Oh. Well, I just wanted to apologize for all the things I told you on Halloween. I didn't want you to think I'm a rotten person."

Can I help it if I believe everything anybody tells me? He said he wasn't a rotten person. So fine, I'll accept that. I inquired about the state of his health, which I knew there must be something wrong with or he'd have been on the stage of the Curran Theatre dancing and singing his little heart out. (That's right —another chorus boy. I told you: in those days I had a *thing* for chorus boys.)

It developed that he was indeed suffering from something that had convinced him that as far as he was concerned, the show didn't have to go on. Being a sucker, I let him talk me into going downtown and doing a Gray Lady routine. I stopped across the street at the funeral parlor long enough to swipe a nice bouquet that didn't look too funereal, check out the makeup on the corpse, and cover the gap in the lineup of floral tributes. On the way downtown I disposed of the sympathy card (Larry, after all, was not dying) and presented myself at the Hotel Divine, a grouping of tawdry rooms lurking above an overpriced deli. Larry was doing a Camille number in the bed, wearing a rather tattered bathrobe. That, as it turned out, was the key to Larry: he was constantly trying to pass off the flannel of his life as silk brocade.

I tossed the bouquet into a corner, poured him a shot of apple juice, and we got down to the business of converting our armed truce into the love affair of the season.

All very romantic.

Within two days we had love eternal, and he had hepatitis. It turned out that the hepatitis was as apocryphal as the love eternal, but we'll get into that later.

For now, suffice it to say that I told Aunt Sylvia that the girl of her dreams turned out to be a chorus boy named Larry. This prompted an immediate reply in which Aunt Sylvia said a few things about dreams turning into nightmares, and demanded a full explanation of exactly what I was talking about. So I sat down and wrote her a letter, which I will reproduce in full, it being what you could call a turning point.

8

Dear Aunt Sylvia,

You asked about Larry, and I got the feeling from your letter that you think I didn't love him. That is not true. As far as I was concerned, he was the sun, and the moon, and the stars, at least for a week or so. He was talented, and interesting, handsome, and charming, a delight to be with. Also an egocentric son-of-a-bitch, but who wasn't?

So there we were on election night, falling in love. For two or three weeks, we were totally inseparable—once Larry got out of the hospital. Also when he wasn't working and I wasn't in school. We were together on the weekends, except for matinees, and in the afternoon for early dinner or late supper, and after the theater for walking and talking and all the things two people who are young and in love do. (Right, Aunt Sylvia, we were doing some of *that,* too.) So what happened? The show left town, and mine wasn't the only broken heart in San Francisco. But it was all right. Larry came back to me three months later.

Closed his apartment in New York, packed up his clothes, and moved to San Francisco.

And that's when the trouble started. Suddenly, from being a minor featured player (chorus boy) in a touring show, he was an unemployed minor featured player (chorus boy) in San Francisco, taking a cab to the unemployment office every other week.

Also, he had nothing to do.

Also, he wasn't willing to do anything that San Francisco had to offer.

Also, he didn't have many friends.

Also, I was going to school.

And I was working in a show downtown, shoving scenery for less than minimum. Do you begin to get the picture?

One thing led to another, and things weren't working out too well. I started staying out after the show. (After all, when he was in a show, he used to go out with everybody afterward. Why shouldn't I?) He started going out to see old movies in Oakland.

Who likes old movies?

Who likes Oakland?

So you can see, our lives were going in different directions. (I always think a touch of melodrama makes a tawdry story such as this more tasteful, don't you?)

I suppose it would have helped if we'd been

willing to talk to each other, but when each party thinks the other one is a stubborn asshole, who's going to talk? We didn't.

Now sit down, Aunt Sylvia, and I will tell you about the night Larry left me. That's right, Aunt Sylvia, someone walked out on your darling little nephew.

It was like this. Larry was off to Oakland for the old movies. (No, I don't know why he had to go to Oakland to see the old movies, but I have my suspicions about that, too.) I went off to play bridge. Except two of the bridge players didn't show up. The extra player and I decided that we might as well go pub-crawling, and hit all the gay bars in town that we'd never been to. You have to remember that this was a long time ago, and there were only about ten bars in town, about five of which Jeff and I had never seen before. It wasn't going to be an extended crawl. I mean, these days, if you want to make an extended crawl of the bars in San Francisco, you can hit twenty in one night, and not even scratch the surface. I hate to think what it will be like in another ten years.

Off we went, winding up at a place that had just opened that night. It was at 333 MacInerny Street, and was imaginatively called the Three-Three-Three Club.

It specialized in leather.

That is to say, it was decorated with leather—leather walls, leather ceiling, leather stools, leather bars, and leather boys. In case you've never seen one, a leather boy is a boy who dresses in leather—leather cap, leather shirt, leather jacket, leather pants, leather underwear (that's right Aunt Sylvia, leather underwear. Believe me, Aunt Sylvia. *I know,* Aunt Sylvia.)

Since it was the opening night, the place was packed. I mean, it smelled like a tannery. Black leather everywhere you looked. Except for Jeff and me and a few other refugees from the Rendezvous who were all gussied up in our fluffy sweaters, tight pants, and tennis shoes. We added a little contrast to the place, anyway.

We made our way in, checked with some friends as to whether a sadist wears his chains on the left and a masochist on the right, or vice versa (I have yet to be absolutely sure of this, so I never get into it with anyone in chains. Rest in peace: scars aren't my scene), and checked the place out. After ten minutes or so we'd more or less had it, but a quick consultation showed that there was no time to get anywhere else before they cut off the booze, so we glommed onto another drink and sat tight.

And then, lo, a party was being organized. Those used to be big things, those after-bar parties. Someone would decide to have a few people in after the bar closed, the address would be passed around, everybody would buy a six-pack, and two or three hundred people would show up for a small do. (One friend of mine managed to throw an after-bar party every Friday and Saturday night for fifty-four consecutive weekends, not counting Christmas. The next tenants in the house used to wonder what the hell was going on when about two thirty every Friday and Saturday night five hundred fairies would come banging on the door wanting to know where Hal was. Hal had chickened out and moved to Oakland, that's where Hal was.)

Anyway, there was a party being organized. Naturally we went. Naturally we assumed it was going to be a normal after-bar party. Naturally we were wrong. It was not a normal after-bar party.

It was an orgy.

That's right, Aunt Sylvia, a genuine, for-real, San Francisco leather crowd orgy.

Aunt Sylvia, you wouldn't have believed it!

It spread through three apartments, and everywhere you looked there were empty beer cans and empty clothes.

Except in the bedrooms, where there were full beer cans and naked men. Fifty of each per bedroom. Multiply that by six bedrooms, and you have an orgy, right? Right!

So what goes on at an orgy? At any normal party everyone gathers in the living room, to pass hors d'oeuvres around. At an orgy everyone gathers in the bedrooms, to pass each other around.

Well, Aunt Sylvia, little Solly was as shocked as you. To me, sex was always a one-on-one proposition. But two-on-one, or three-on-one, or four-on-five? Nossir, not for little Solly Steinberg. I cleared out, dragging Jeff along with me, once I got him out from under the pile. (Jeff, it turned out, was an old hand at this sort of bash.)

We toddled on home, Jeff bragging all the way about how many times he'd been banged, and me wondering what I was going to tell Larry. Finally I decided to tell him the truth. After all, we didn't have any secrets from each other, did we? We loved each other, didn't we? He'd understand, wouldn't he?

No, on all counts.

What happened was this. He was waiting for me, fuming. So I told him where I'd been. He *must* have heard the word "orgy," but I'd swear to this day that the slamming of the front door coincided with it exactly. That was the last I saw of Larry for several days. Not the last I *heard* from him, but the last I saw of him. He'd come sneaking in when he knew I wasn't there to pick up his mail and leave obscene notes.

So what happened, you're asking? Naturally, after three days I went to see some friends to find out if they'd heard from Larry.

Naturally they hadn't.

Naturally I sat there and told them everything.

Naturally Larry was sitting upstairs listening to every incriminating word. So what's the moral? Never trust your friends, that's the moral!

Larry decided to come home, eventually, since nobody else would put up with him and the rent was paid till the first, and we had a long Truth Session. Turned out Larry was a few years older than he'd been claiming to be, and had been going off to the baths to get his rocks off regularly since he'd been living with me.

With this straightened out, we decided to put it back together again. (Remember, the rent was paid till the first of the month.) Putting it together again involved fighting regularly, and, well, doing something else just as regularly, but it turned out I was a lot better at the fighting than the something else. An impasse was reached.

You remember I went traveling that summer? Larry did not go with me. Instead he got a job playing minor featured parts (chorus boy) at some broken-down music tent in the East Bay, and moved to Oakland.

There he met Another Man, and I got a Dear Solly letter, only it was addressed to Murray.

I'm pleased to report that Another Man, though he lasted four years, didn't fare any better than I did, and the last time I saw Larry, he was selling books over the counter on Hollywood Boulevard. *Sic transit* Larry.

Let me tell you, Aunt Sylvia, marriage is not all that great. Are you starting to get the picture?

Love,
Solly

As I said earlier, sending this letter was not the smartest thing I ever did.

9

Aunt Sylvia's reply was for some reason delayed for a couple of days, and when it arrived, I knew immediately that the shit was about to hit whatever it is shit hits. The letter ran to two pages, which for Aunt Sylvia is a major effort. She is usually able to pack the weekly dosage of recriminations into one or two concise paragraphs, but obviously she was beginning to get desperate. . . .

Dear Solomon, [Right away, you know it's trouble!]

I checked with Uncle Hymie, and he says that two men cannot get married. Also, he wanted to know why I asked, so I showed him your last letter. He is coming to visit you. In the meantime, I want you to know that I have been doing some reading about people like who you say you are like, and I can't believe you are really like that.

So you must be going through a phase. But that's all right—you've gone through phases before. You wet your bed till you were thirteen years old, but it passed. All things pass, Solly. Keep that in mind.

I was talking to Hymie's sister Sarah last week, before your letter arrived, and she asked me when you were getting married. So I told her you *were* married, but for some reason had felt you couldn't tell us about it (remember I thought she might be a shiksa?), but that it was all going to be all right now, and when you brought your wife to visit us I'd have her and Abe over for dinner. What do you think I ought to tell her now? Shall I tell her you got a divorce? Or shall I tell her it was just some of your *mishegaas*? I guess I'd better talk to Uncle Hymie about it.

There isn't a lot of news, as I've been spending a good deal of time in bed lately. I don't want you should feel guilty, but it seems like my attacks coincide with the arrival of your letters. I'm sure there's no connection, but I'm going to see Rachel Pomerantz's son the doctor about it next week.

Your Uncle Hymie will arrive at San Francisco airport next Friday night on flight 612. Be sure to pick him up because he doesn't like to take the bus into town. He'll stay at the Jack Tar unless you can put him up. Can you? Don't feel you have to just because he's your uncle who raised you. He'll be perfectly all right at the hotel, although I think their room service stops at two in the morning and I don't know how Hymie will get his medicine if anything happens to him in the night. But I'm sure he'll manage. He'll come back on Sunday night so he can get to work on Monday morning. He wants to retire, but we have to think of the future, don't we?

Take care of yourself, Solly, and stop being what you are. You'll be much happier, and so will I.

Love,
Aunt Sylvia

Uncle Hymie is coming up here? Why is Uncle Hymie coming up here? What am I saying—I *know* why Uncle Hymie is coming up here, and I wish he would stay at home. However, I also know that if Aunt Sylvia wants him to come up here, he'll come up here.

I figured if he was coming up, he might as well stay with me, so I checked my calendar, and where I was going to write "Uncle Hymie," there was already something written. "Party @ 200" is what it said. Suddenly it seemed that maybe the hotel would be better after all. But the Jack Tar? It isn't even on the right side of Van Ness! Couldn't he stay at the Fairmont? Or the Hyatt Regency? I quickly began making the necessary arrangements.

I arranged for Uncle Hymie to be on the sixteenth floor of the Hyatt Regency, with a nice view of the Bay and Berkeley. Also, if he gets too upset by whatever might happen during our visit, he can always step across the hall and plunge to his death in the lobby.

I telephoned Aunt Sylvia to let her know I was doing all the things I should be doing, and she told me that I shouldn't plan anything for the weekend, because Uncle Hymie wants to have breakfast with me on Saturday.

Breakfast on Saturday? *Nobody* eats breakfast on Saturday. Brunch on Sunday, perhaps, but breakfast on Saturday? Yech! Also, of course, there is the fact that I am going to be in the kitchen all day Saturday ("Party @ 200") trying to figure out how to feed the masses. It's not easy feeding two hundred hungry men, and if any dykes show up, I don't know what I'll do. (Not that I've invited any, but with a party this size you never know who will show up. There was one a couple of years ago that suddenly got invaded by what seemed to be the Hell's Angels, but it turned out to be all right —they were only a stockbroker, a CPA, and a Southern Baptist minister in leather drag. . . .)

Anyway, I told Aunt Sylvia I'd pick Uncle Hymie up at the airport, buy him a drink, and install him at the hotel. I also told her he was welcome to come to the party on Saturday night, but if he didn't want to I'd get him some theater tickets. (I still know a couple of chorus boys—getting older but still working.)

Then I told her I was sorry she'd been spending so much time in bed, and that I got the feeling she was trying to inflict some guilt on me. Before she had a chance to say anything, I told her to forget it—five years of therapy cost me a lot of cash, but it also taught me a thing or two—namely that I'm quite capable of whipping up my own guilt, and that I don't need hers. Then I hung up the phone before she could give me some anyway.

I spent the rest of the week next to the mailbox, waiting for the letter that Aunt Sylvia was sure to write. It didn't come, and by Friday morning I was beginning to think everything might work out all right. On the other hand, there's something they say about mice and men, and I guess it applies to fairies, too. . . .

10

I picked Uncle Hymie up at the airport as promised.
I was a little late, since I had to walk Mitzie and Fritzie,
and I ran into an old friend, and you know how that
goes. We started talking, and one thing led to another.
I got to the airport thirty minutes late. I found Uncle
Hymie waiting for the bus into town, and piled him
into my car. He didn't seem too pleased at being kept
waiting, but by the time we got into the city he'd
calmed down enough to say hello. I glanced over at
him, keeping one eye on the road.

"I suppose Aunt Sylvia put you up to this?" I asked.

"Up to what?" Uncle Hymie growled.

"This visit."

"What about it?"

"Uncle Hymie," I said, trying to sound forceful, "I
know why you're here."

He finally looked at me, but with a sort of strained
look on his face.

"Solly, if you know why I'm here, I wish you'd tell
me about it."

"Maybe we'd better wait till we get to the hotel," I said, showing the usual amount of Steinberg courage.

Conversation was minimal after that, me concentrating on getting us to the hotel, and Uncle Hymie concentrating on God knows what.

So we got to the hotel, and I think it was the first time I ever saw Uncle Hymie really impressed with something. I mean, he stared, looking at the stream, and the trees, and those things that buzz up and down the walls looking like something Queen Victoria might have used for an outhouse. We got him checked in, stuck his stuff in his room, and I decided to face up to things. I mean, I figured Aunt Sylvia'd sent him up here for a confrontation, so I decided to have the confrontation.

I suggested we go to the bar.

Uncle Hymie suggested we go for dinner.

I said I had a date for dinner.

Uncle Hymie wanted to know who with.

With a friend. (Am I going to make it easy? Not me! Besides, the friend I'm having dinner with is Scott Harney, who is not exactly designed to reassure the heart of an uncertain uncle. I mean, Scotty is a good person, and all that, but he tends to drink a bit much, and he hates to have his non-working life loused up with straight people. Scotty liberated himself years ago, when he moved from Denver to San Francisco, and likes to claim that, outside of working hours, which he thinks are a legitimate exemption, he hasn't spoken to a single straight person in three years. Personally, I don't think he can be so sure—I mean, you can't always spot a heterosexual when you see one, can you? It's not like they wear signs, or anything.)

"He'll mind if the uncle who raised you joins you?" said Uncle Hymie.

"Well," I hedged, "I don't know . . ."

"What kind of friend is that? You call him and tell him your uncle is in town. and I'll blow both of you to the whole thing."

I don't think he really meant "blow," but what the hell. So we went to dinner. I don't know what Uncle Hymie was expecting, but for the first twenty minutes he was very quiet. So were Scotty and I. That's when I really began to worry: when Uncle Hymie gets quiet like that you never know what he's going to say. But he said it. Eventually, he said it.

"Solly, I don't see any girls in here," he said.

"It's not that kind of place, Uncle Hymie," I said.

"What kind of place is it?" he said.

"It's what you call a gay restaurant," I said.

"And they don't let girls in?" he wanted to know.

"It's not that. It's just that the girls don't come here very often. They have their own places," I finished, a bit lamely.

The evening wasn't exactly loaded with scintillating conversation. Scott sat there looking uncomfortable, wanting to tell me all the gory details of his latest affair, but let's face it—how could he be frank with Uncle Hymie sitting there trying to figure out what was going on? So we all sat there, drearily pushing our food into our mouths. A restaurant it was; gay it wasn't, not that Friday night. Anyway, we finished dinner, and I began to think it was time for Uncle Hymie to go back to the hotel.

"What's next?" said Uncle Hymie.

"Next?" It was beginning to look like a horrible evening was closing in.

"Where do we go from here?"

"Well, I thought you'd probably want to go back to the hotel. . . ."

Uncle Hymie folded his napkin carefully, and drank some coffee. Here it comes, I thought.

"Solly, I've been thinking. Your Aunt Sylvia made me come up here, and I have to admit, I was not averse to the idea. I mean, who wants a queer in the family? So I'm supposed to talk sense to you. Make you see the error of your ways. But it occurs to me: I don't know your ways. I don't know anything about you. So if I'm going to talk sense to you, I'd better find out a few things. I mean, I look around this restaurant, Solly, and do I see queers? I don't see what I always thought were queers. If you put a few women in here, most all these guys would look normal."

"What makes you think they're not?" Scotty put in. (Scotty's very high on Gay Lib, and doesn't let much get past him.)

Uncle Hymie peered at Scotty over his glasses for a few minutes, and seemed to think the question over.

"So what's normal?" he said at last. "All my life I thought I was normal and I thought Solly was normal. So maybe I was wrong. But maybe I'm not wrong. I want to find out. So if it's all right with you two, you just go ahead with your Friday night, and I'll sort of tag along and pick up the checks. God knows I paid enough for Solly's education. I might as well spend some on my own."

Well, you have to admit, that was quite a speech. Scott stared at me with a sort of "Murray, what have you gotten us into?" look, and I just sat there. I mean, spending Friday night letting Uncle Hymie use me as an educational aid was not what I had had in mind.

Getting laid was what I had had in mind, and Scott and I had a nice program mapped out—first hit a few bars, starting on Polk Street, then working our way into the raunchier districts, ending up at two in the morning in one of the tawdrier bars south of Market, where all's well that ends well if you're not too fussy about keeping your pants on. Also, if all else failed, we planned a quick trip to the steambaths after two. (To sober up, of course.)

I could see in Scott's face that Uncle Hymie was not going to fit into these plans, but what could I do? I tried to talk him out of it, really I did, but everywhere we went we had at least one drink, and every time we ran into friends, they set us up to a round, and—well, maybe I'd better take it chronologically. It got a little confusing as the night wore on.

Scott and I had a quick consultation while Uncle Hymie settled the check, and decided that the C.Q. was a good place to start. Piano bar, lots of atmosphere, female singer (*real* female), and nothing blatantly felonious going on. How were we to know they were having a toga party that night? Nobody told *us*. As we arrived, nothing much was happening except that a lion was wandering along the sidewalk asking all the Christians if they'd like to be eaten. I stuck my head in the door and things looked pretty quiet, so we went in. We found three stools at the piano bar and sat down with our backs to the room, which I felt was a shrewd move, tactically speaking. What Uncle Hymie doesn't see doesn't shock him, right?

Everything went swimmingly for the first few minutes: a fat broad sang "Penny Candy" and "Put Your Head on My Pillow," which brought tears to the eyes of a couple of gin-soaked piss-elegant numbers with hair dyed to match their camel-hair coats, and Scott and I began to breathe a little easier. That's when the waiter, who's an old friend (I know him intimately, if not well) comes over to take the order.

"Murray!" he peals. "Guess what I have on under this toga?"

Well, I was pretty sure I knew what he had on, and I was pretty sure he was about to show me, so I whirled around to block Uncle Hymie. Too late. The waiter already had his skirt up, and Uncle Hymie had proof that not only nice Jewish boys are gay. Uncle Hymie's eyes popped a bit—the waiter *is* hung like a horse— but he managed not to say anything. Perhaps he was speechless. I looked severely at the waiter, made some silly gesture in Hymie's direction, and the toga fell back into place as the order was taken. Scott and I put away three while Uncle Hymie sipped his Scotch. Uncle Hymie looked like he needed three, but I guess he doesn't believe in drinking while he's studying.

We left just as the Empress de San Francisco made her entrance. She's a six-foot Mexican transvestite who likes to throw barstools around when anyone hinted that she wasn't every inch a lady. She wasn't, and someone always hinted. That particular night she happened to have her tiara on upside down, and that, mixed with several drinks too many, was bound to cause a scene. As I said, we left.

Across the street and down a block is the Hot Spot, but we figured it wouldn't be too hot for Uncle Hymie, who's still trying to figure out what to say to a naked waiter. Organ music and dancing is their thing, but Uncle Hymie wasn't impressed. At least he wasn't impressed by the old queen who wanted to dance with him. I explained that Uncle Hymie wasn't exactly into dancing with men, and the old queen apologized, mentioned that there was some question concerning the validity of his manhood but under the circumstances what-the-hell, and bought us a round of drinks. Then he asked Uncle Hymie if he'd like to go home and fuck.

I must say I was proud of Uncle Hymie. No seizures, no attack, no sputtering. All he did was look the old number over, shake his head, and say "I didn't know people our age *could* go home and fuck."

The old queen shook his head sadly.

"My word, he *is* straight, isn't he?" he muttered, and staggered off to find someone more entertaining to spend his money on. Uncle Hymie became very quiet for a while.

Scott and I had several more drinks.

Uncle Hymie paid the check.

That's the way it went for a while. Scott and I got drunker and drunker, and Uncle Hymie's education got a few extras thrown in. Somewhere along the line we decided that Uncle Hymie really ought to see how the other half lives, so we took him south of Market.

I should mention here, I suppose, that there are all kinds of gay people, and one group doesn't mix with another any more than one kind of straight group mixes with another. For me, going south of Market is slumming; for them, going north of Market is slumming. However, Scott and I were drunk, and Uncle Hymie, I guess, was in a mood to "go to Harlem," so off we went to Folsom Street. That's where the leather-and-chains crowd hangs out, and as I think I may have mentioned, I've never been sure what means what where chains are concerned. However, it's fun to watch.

We warned Uncle Hymie to stay out of all dark corners and back rooms, and headed for the Raunch Room, which, while not on Folsom Street, is the definitive Folsom Street bar. Nice little place, if you like people who dress tough, talk opera, and collect crystal. Also, that's where Uncle Hymie ran into an old friend of his.

Aunt Sylvia knows him, too. His name is Sam Levitz, and he lives in Tarzana with his wife, Miriam, and their four kids. He sells dress material wholesale, but it seems that Sam likes leather better than knits. There he was, lounging at the bar, a beer clutched in one hand, his thumb hooked in a keychain, when in comes our little threesome.

"Oy vay," says Uncle Hymie. "That looks like Sam Levitz."

"Maybe it is," I say.

"Nah. Sam Levitz lives in Tarzana, has four kids, and sells dress material wholesale," says Uncle Hymie.

"Hymie!" says Sam Levitz.

"Let's get out of here," says Uncle Hymie.

"Too late," says Scott. "Is he supposed to be straight?"

"Is that drag?" says me.

By now Sam has gotten to us. From the look of him, he's been putting away the beer pretty fast. Also, for a dress-material salesman from Tarzana, he's dressed pretty funny—a leather cap, with lots of buttons on it advertising gay bars and motorcycle runs (the leather crowd likes to travel in packs and go on picnics), leather jacket open to the waist with no shirt to cover his hairy chest (the leather crowd likes to show chests, the hairier the better), filthy blue jeans with the crotch sanded to make it look like his cock is so big it's wearing through his pants, motorcycle boots, and a chain dog collar on his right ankle.

"What's the dog collar for, Sam?" says Uncle Hymie, getting straight to the point.

"Dog collar? What dog collar?"

"On your ankle."

"I'm an 'M,' " says Sam.

"I always thought you were Reform," says Hymie.

"It has nothing to do with religion," says Sam.

"And that's a pretty weird yarmulkah," adds Uncle Hymie. "What's going on, Sam?"

"I might ask you the same thing," says Sam, starting to look a little wary.

"I came up to visit Solly, here, and he and his friend are showing me around."

Now Sam looks very wary. "So you came out to look at the freaks?"

"Are you a freak?" asks Uncle Hymie.

"He just looks like one," Scott puts in, hoping nobody will hear. (It's not considered good taste to cast aspersions on the leather set when they're clearly in the majority. Not unless you want your white shoes scuffed and your sweater frayed.)

By now Sam Levitz is looking pretty worried. I mean, here he is, mixing with the natives as it were, in what could not by any stretch of the imagination be called a straight bar. Not only is he mixing with the natives, he looks like one, and any chance of passing himself off as a tourist is being wrecked by the fact that everybody seems to know him.

Also, he keeps groping friends as they greet him.

Probably a reflex, but certainly not geared to convince Uncle Hymie that it's all a coincidence. Uncle Hymie is finding out that anybody can be gay, even

Sam Levitz who lives in Tarzana and has four children and sells dress material wholesale.

"You come here often?" Uncle Hymie finally ventures. Sam throws in the towel.

"Only when I'm in town."

Uncle Hymie nods. "I can see how Miriam might not understand. She give you that outfit for your birthday?"

"I bought it myself." Now Sam is looking very unhappy. "You won't mention this to Miriam, will you?"

Uncle Hymie shakes his head. "I tell Miriam where I saw you, I admit where I was. Now, if you who come here don't want it mentioned, you think I'm going to talk it around that I was here? I got a reputation, too, you know."

Sam relaxes. He even becomes expansive, if that is a word that can be ascribed to an aging rag merchant whose beer-filled gut is beginning to hang over his studded belt.

"So, Hymie, what brings you to town?"

"The kid here"—he jerks his thumb at me—"told Sylvia he's queer, so I'm finding out what it's all about."

"What have you found out?"

"So far only that you guys tend to dress a little weird sometimes, but nobody seems to mind, and if everybody's happy who cares?"

"Too bad there aren't more like you in the world," says Sam, a little wistfully.

"Maybe if you gave people a chance . . ." Uncle Hymie begins.

"You stick your neck out, you get your head cut off," Sam replies.

"Solly stuck his out, and so far it still seems to be attached."

"Solly is a decorator, Solly lives in San Francisco, and Solly isn't married," Sam points out.

"So what happened to you?" Uncle Hymie wants to know.

"I didn't even know what gay was till I was forty. By then it was too late. So now I'm me every third weekend. The rest of the time it's the Sam Levitz you all know and love."

There was a long silence. Sam seemed to have taken the glow off the party. Scott sidled over to the bar to place an order, and I glanced around to see who else might be lurking in the gloom. By now, everyone in our immediate vicinity had started listening to our conversation, so things were pretty quiet. Uncle Hymie broke the silence.

"Sam, I'm sorry."

"Sorry?"

"Sorry for you, sorry for Miriam, sorry for the kids. What are you going to do?"

"I should do something?"

"How long can you go on this way?"

"Fourteen years so far. Maybe after the kids are grown . . ."

"What about Miriam?"

"She doesn't suspect a thing."

"She doesn't know *any*thing?"

"It would kill her."

"How's the sex life at home?"

"What sex life at home? There hasn't been any for years."

"And Miriam doesn't know why?"

"She thinks I'm impotent."

"She should see you in that outfit. You don't look impotent to me, Sam-boy."

[56]

We didn't stay much longer at the Raunch Room: I think Uncle Hymie was afraid he was spoiling Sam's evening out with the boys. By now it was after midnight, and Hymie, thank God, was starting to feel his age.

"Any place else you boys were thinking of going?" he asked.

"Home," I said. "Lots to do tomorrow."

"From what I saw, I'd say you guys usually stay out a lot later than this. That last place was just getting filled up. I oughta open up a queer bar: they must make a fortune."

"Gay bar," Scott corrected him. "And they do, but not for straight people."

"Be gay, buy gay?"

"Something like that," Scott said.

"So what did you think?" I asked.

"About what?" asked cagey Uncle Hymie.

"What you saw."

"Solly, what I saw tonight is more new things than I've ever seen in any one night in my life. You expect me to have thought about it all, too? Take me to the hotel, I'm gonna go to bed and think."

So we took him back to the hotel, and he went to bed to think. He must have thought a lot, because I didn't hear from him at all the next day. Not till he showed up at the party. God, did he show up at the party!

11

Uncle Hymie didn't call all the next day, but that was all right—I was up to my tits in hot hors d'oeuvres, anyway.

The party was going to be one of those open-house-from-four-till-eight things, which in San Francisco means nobody shows up before seven thirty, and at two o'clock in the morning they're still arriving. What the hell—nobody works on Sunday anyway, and one can always go directly from the party to brunch, the baths, or whatever.

So at four o'clock, who shows up? Right. Uncle Hymie. I'm still in my housedress, hair in curlers, and no makeup. In other words, I haven't shaved yet.

Am I ready for Uncle Hymie?

No, I'm not ready for Uncle Hymie. Also, Uncle Hymie is wearing a business suit.

"Going back to L.A.?" I asked him.

"Coming to the party," he said, peering around. "Am I the first?"

"You'd better be. I'm counting on nobody showing up till at least seven thirty."

"I thought it was four to eight."

"It is. San Francisco time. But it's all right, because you can't wear that suit anyway."

"What's wrong with this suit? I got it at J. C. Penney."

"That's the first thing. But mainly, nobody is going to be wearing suits. You'll feel ridiculous."

"So what should I wear?"

"What have you got?" I countered.

"Another suit."

I thought it over. On the one hand, I didn't have time to go shopping with Uncle Hymie, and on the other hand I didn't want him to be embarrassed at the party. So I gave him my credit card to The Natural Man, and sent him down to Polk Street. Then I called the shop, told the manager that my Uncle Hymie would be in and he should put him into something nice for a Sixties Nostalgia party, and started hauling myself together. That is not as easy as it sounds. It goes something like this:

Mix a drink.

Crawl upstairs to the bedroom, and open the closet door.

Begin making selections of what to wear. This may sound simple, but it isn't. First, one has to decide on one's image for the evening. With Sixties Nostalgia, you have choices. One can go piss-elegant, and wear something simple in black velvet (I have a nice jumpsuit in black velvet with the seams studded with rhinestones. Good for opening night at the opera, but not much else.) Or casual trashy, which involves pre-worn

Levi's jeans (at thirty-six dollars a shot) with a matching jacket (fifty dollars). Then there are all the degrees in between, ranging from pants and sport shirt (known as sweaters-and-skirts in my crowd) to a tux (high drag). Or one can always go the whole hog, and actually *get* in drag. With only a couple of hours, though, that's out of the question: I can barely get my hair combed in a couple of hours.

After clawing through about sixty or seventy possible outfits, I decided another drink was definitely in order, and that the project was too major to attempt alone. So I called Scotty:

"Scotty? Murray. Are you pulled together yet?" (Dumb question—Scotty is one of those people who's always pulled together. Give him three minutes, and he's ready for a garden party at Buckingham Palace, whether or not the party's ready for him.)

"I was just leaving. I thought you might need some help."

"I do. I don't have a damned thing to wear, so you pick out something chic while I get the wrecking crew in to do something with the body. I've decided to simply write the face off as a total loss and turn down all the lights."

"If it's going to be an orgy, I'll bring a towel."

"Forget it. Uncle Hymie's coming."

"Oh, shit. Does that mean I can't grope?"

"Only in the bathroom, which is where you generally spend most of your time anyway. Get your ass over here—I'll leave the door open."

I hung up the phone, stirred up another drink, and went back upstairs to count the wrinkles.

Halfway through the inventory Scott arrived, fixed himself a drink, and appeared in the bathroom door.

"Still counting? Why don't you just assign them each a number, make up a checklist, and get the job done fast?"

"It's friendlier this way. Besides, if I stare at them long enough, I know exactly what I have to pretend doesn't exist. Also, I know that the tricks are interested in me, not my once-pretty face. Go find something for me to wear. I'll be out in about ten."

"*In* about ten or *at* about ten?" he sneered.

He disappeared, and I began the process of cleaning up. I know a shower and shave shouldn't take an hour, but one thing leads to another, and that's the way things are. Two drinks later, the job was done. I staggered into the bedroom. Scott was up to his ass in clothes.

"What am I wearing?" I asked, not really caring.

"This," Scott said with a tone of finality.

What he was holding was something I bought one day on the off-chance that I would have to make an appearance at a formal dedication of an Arabian oil well. Besides, I'm a freak for gold lamé (who among us isn't?) and the brocade trim alone was worth the price of the garment ($450).

"Surely you jest," I said, knowing damn well that he didn't.

"Well, you ought to wear it once before it rots off the hanger, and God knows you can't wear it out."

"It'll *never* wear out," I complained.

"That's not what I meant."

"You've worn worse."

"Too true. Anyway, it's very hostessy, and since this is your party you ought to wear it."

"I'll look like a kike."

"You are a kike, darling. Get into it. You don't happen to have any beaded slippers, do you? They'd go perfectly."

I glowered at him, and crawled into the thing. He zipped it up and stepped back.

"Tell you what. Don't move till I get you another drink. By then you won't care anymore."

"What do I look like?"

"Does anybody here want to fuck an aging Jewish lesbian?"

"Oh, God," I said, and reached for the zipper. Needless to say, it jammed.

"Get me that other drink, while I get this thing fixed."

Scott headed downstairs, and I fiddled with the zipper. Eventually he returned, and I began drinking the drink and working with the zipper. Scott was right; by the time I finished the drink, I didn't care anymore.

"What the hell," I said. "Should I wear anything under it?"

"With the zipper jammed, it doesn't matter. But if you invite anyone to spend the night, warn him that he's going to have trouble undressing you."

"I'll just pull the whole thing up over my head, and he won't have to look at my face."

"If he looks at your face, he won't stay."

"Too true. Let's go down and prepare for the teeming hordes."

By seven, I was more or less ready, and at seven thirty, the party began. The first arrival was the manager of The Natural Man.

"Murray," he said, "what are you trying to do to me?"

"I sent you some business. Be happy."

"Darling, I'm sure your Uncle Hymie is a marvelous man, but he simply has no taste in clothes."

"What did you expect? He's straight."

Charles looked stricken. "Jesus, darling, you didn't *tell* me that."

"Well, I figured you'd assume—"

"Never figure I'll assume anything. It's been so long since I've seen a straight man that I've forgotten what they look like."

"They look like Uncle Hymie."

"Not anymore they don't," Charles muttered, heading for the bar. I grabbed his arm.

"Charles. What, exactly, did you sell Uncle Hymie?"

"You'll know soon enough. He's straight, hunh?"

"Very."

"Well, maybe that explains why he insisted on the full-length raincoat."

"Raincoat?"

"After I got him all set for the party, and had everything boxed up, he insisted on buying a full-length raincoat."

"What on earth for?"

"Well, love," Charles purred, "if I were straight, and if I were going to go out wearing what your Uncle Hymie is going to be wearing tonight, I'd want a raincoat too. To cover it all up with."

With that, Charles shook off my hand, squared his shoulders, and made it to the bar.

Uncle Hymie didn't show up till about nine thirty, and frankly I give him a medal for courage. *I* wouldn't have shown up at all. But he came.

There were about thirty people there when he arrived, and I was more or less monitoring the door.

The bell rang, and there stood Uncle Hymie in his full-length raincoat. He stared at me.

"You're wearing a dress?" he asked.

"It's a caftan, Uncle Hymie."

"It looks like a dress."

"Take my word for it. It's a caftan. So they look better on the models—what can I tell you?"

"You want I should take off my coat?" Hymie asked.

"Only if you want to."

"I don't know what kind of store that was you sent me to, but they sure have some strange clothes," he said, unbuttoning the raincoat.

What Charles had done to Uncle Hymie shouldn't be done to a dog. Uncle Hymie is not what you could call bald, at least not on his body. Well, Charles had put him into one of those fishnet shirts that look so good on the Arnold Schwarzenegger types. On Uncle Hymie, the effect was a little different. The hair was tufted through the fishnet, and so was Uncle Hymie's fat. He looked like one of those huge sausages you see in Italian markets; definitely not kosher.

Below the belt, which was metal, he was wearing a pair of elephant-bell pants, and when you consider that Uncle Hymie's waist is about fifty, you can imagine how big the bell-bottoms were. It looked like a pair of paisley coulottes, and Charles had bottomed the whole thing out with a pair of four-inch platforms rising to six inches at the heel. Around his neck he had a scarf fastened with a huge amethyst slide. Since the shoes were made out of purple plastic, I suppose the amethyst was supposed to tie the outfit together. I looked him over.

"Well?" he said.

"You look taller."

"That all you got to say?"

"How do you feel?"

"About how Sam Levitz looked last night. Weird."

"That's how you look," I agreed. "I'd offer you something else, but I don't have anything that'd fit. Unless you want to wear a caftan."

"Thanks, but no thanks. At least this isn't a dress. Can I have a drink?"

"The bar's over there. And if you feel like picking a fight with Charles, be my guest."

So Uncle Hymie wandered off to the bar, and I began to get a little nervous. The room was filling up, and so far, no girls.

No girls, you're asking? At a party like that, what does he want girls for?

Well, let me tell you. What can happen is this: gay men tend to be interesting people. But they also tend to be horny. So, if there are no women around, the interesting conversation soon becomes an interesting conversation about sex. That gets all the horny men even hornier, and all of a sudden you notice that a couple of people have disappeared. Then a couple more. Eventually all the bedrooms are full, the bathrooms are overcrowded, and the corners of the living room are starting to get a little lively. I'm not complaining, of course. I've got nothing against an orgy. It's just that I hadn't planned one for that particular night, and I didn't see that Uncle Hymie needed a lesson in *exactly* what gay people do as part of his education. So, I'm keeping one eye on the door and the other one on the crowd. So far, things are going fairly well. Uncle Hymie is circulating, and the word is out that he's my straight uncle from Beverly Hills.

Everyone's being nice. On the other hand, everyone's still sober. I give Scott the high sign.

"How's it look?" I ask.

"So far, so good. Except that Rita-Rose is getting a bad case of hot pants."

"Rita-Rose *always* has a bad case of hot pants. Who's the lucky one tonight?"

"Guess."

"Uncle Hymie?" I say, seeing my party about to be destroyed. I mean, I've seen Rita-Rose in action before, and when that queen sets her cap for someone, the someone has two choices; give in, or get out. Rita has been on the make for at least forty years, and it always follows a pattern. He gets very attentive, and starts getting drinks for the intended victim. But Rita always drinks right along with the victim, and Rita doesn't hold his liquor very well. This wouldn't be too bad, except that when Rita gets drunk, he gets explicit about what he wants. Which wouldn't be too bad either, except that it looked like he was about to start getting explicit with Uncle Hymie. That looked bad. I thought the situation over.

"How would you like to do me a big favor?" I asked Scott.

"If you mean how would I like to make a play for Rita-Rose, I wouldn't. I've been avoiding her for years."

"One of us has to," I countered, "and I'm the host. I can't devote all my time to one guest."

"You've done it before."

"But the guest wasn't Rita-Rose."

"It's still a precedent. Besides, it's your party, your guest, and *your* Uncle Hymie. And if Rita gets too drunk, it will be your disaster."

[66]

"All right, I'll make you a deal. I'll decoy Rita and you go upstairs and call every dyke you know. If we can get a mess of lesbians in here, Rita will leave."

"So will everyone else."

"Better that than having Rita ask Uncle Hymie to pee on her. That I couldn't face."

"Why don't you just kick her out?"

"Last time I did that she got mad and reported a fire here. Who knows what she might do this time?"

So Scott went upstairs, and I sidled over to Rita, who was busily plying Uncle Hymie with drinks.

"Murray," Rita cooed, "you never told me you had such an adorable uncle. He's simply divine."

"Also straight, Rita. Why don't you get me a drink?"

"You? You've never let me buy you a drink in your life."

"Here you don't have to buy it for me. It's my liquor."

"Well, you know what I mean."

"I know what you mean, but times change. If it'll make you feel better, leave a dollar fifty on the bar."

Rose lit up like a church and skidded off to the bar.

"He's a weird one," Uncle Hymie commented.

"Oh?" I said as noncommittally as possible.

"Says he wants to take me home and have me pee on him."

"Oh, Christ."

"He really likes that?"

"He really does."

"Well, if that's his bag . . . is 'bag' the right word?"

"Uncle Hymie, didn't that upset you?"

"Should it?"

"Well . . ."

"Look, Solly, there are lots of men who want that sort of thing from women. So he wants it from another man. So what? You think you gay people have a corner on strange sex? You should hear some of the things that go on in Beverly Hills."

Well, I have to admit that there was a thought that had never crossed my mind. All these years of being told how weird we queers are, and now here's Uncle Hymie laying it on me that the straights aren't so straight themselves. Let's hear it for one hundred million heterosexual felons!

Just as I'm about to propose a toast to the perverts of Beverly Hills (may they go forth and multiply), Scott comes crashing down the stairs and into the room.

"It's all right," he crows. "Reinforcements are on the way. Three P.E. teachers and a car-wash manager."

Heads turn.

Ice clinks.

Mutters are muttered.

"Jesus, they invited lesbians."

"If I'd wanted to spend the evening with men, I'd have gone to the ball game."

"I hope they're not armed."

"*I* hope they're not *drunk.*"

"By the time they get here, *we'd* better be."

"I though Murray had more sense."

"She gets carried away."

"She must have a late date, and wants us all out of here."

"For Christ's sake!" I shouted. "They're only women."

"Darling," someone purred, "you may think they're

women, and Christ may think they're women, but *they* think they're men. Where's my coat?"

I watched about half my party leave, simply because I wanted to protect Uncle Hymie from Rita-Rose. I'll never try to protect Uncle Hymie again. Next time, he can protect himself. At least I was rid of Rita.

The girls arrived, and they weren't nearly as bad as everybody thought they would be, except for the car-wash manager, who was worse. It wouldn't have been so bad if she'd kept her pants on, but she kept stripping down to her jockey shorts and asking everybody to "check her basket." I hope the ceiling was clean, because every square inch of it got examined. I tried to keep an eye on Uncle Hymie, but by then I'd more or less stopped worrying—he seemed to be able to take care of himself, and if anything was upsetting him he didn't show it.

Eventually things seemed to calm down, and we were standing around in little groups, the men swapping recipes and the girls talking shop—all quiet—when comes a pounding on the door.

Cops.

That's right! Five of San Francisco's finest, all jammed up into my doorway like so many blue sardines.

"Are you Murray Roberts?" the front one demanded.

My first thought was to deny it. After all, I'm not *really* Murray Roberts. Not legally, anyway. On the other hand, Murray Roberts is the name on the mailbox, and I'm answering the door. Then again, Roberts could have moved. But why bother? It looked like the fine hand of Rita-Rose was stirring shit, as the phrase goes.

"What's the problem?" I asked, ducking the issue.

"A report of an orgy and drug abuse at this address."

Rita-Rose, I thought.

"Who reported it?"

"May we come in?" asked the front man, also ducking the question.

Now here, I'm going to have to tell you something. If I were straight, I'd have demanded to see a search warrant, and closed the door in their faces if they didn't produce one. But I'm not straight, and I learned long ago that gay people don't have equal rights under the law. Hell, up until a couple of years ago we didn't have *any* rights! I mean, if a straight person calls the police and reports a prowler, what happens? They send out a car, right? Of course, right! If I call and report a prowler, they tell me it's probably an old trick, and don't call us, we'll call you. Also the big butch cops like to beat up on the fairies, but that's not what this is about.

Anyway, I let them in, since I knew there was no orgy going on (who wants to have a gang-bang with four lesbians?) and I certainly didn't keep drugs on the premises. Also, my Uncle Hymie, who has an impeccable reputation, was there, right? All right, so I'd forgotten how he was dressed.

It killed the party, I'll tell you that. You could see everybody wishing he was somewhere else, like maybe Angkor Wat, all except Uncle Hymie, who's a nice, respectable, heterosexual citizen with nothing to hide.

Do you know what happens when the cops come to a party? If it's a straight party, they smile nicely, ask you to keep the noise down, and go on their merry way. If it's a gay party, they collect everybody's identification, then spend a lot of time checking things out to see if they can't bust someone for an old parking ticket. And it doesn't do any good to claim you don't have an I.D. because then they take you in as a vagrant and things really get ugly.

Which is why Uncle Hymie is suing the police department for false arrest.

12

Somehow or another, which I may or may not choose to talk about later, I got Uncle Hymie home on schedule. I figured the best thing to do was simply let him tell Aunt Sylvia whatever he wanted to, and do my best to forget the whole thing. Except that two days after Uncle Hymie went home, I got a letter. . . .

Dear Solly, [Apparently Uncle Hymie didn't tell her much!]

Your Uncle Hymie is back, and I don't know what happened up there—he won't say. He only said he had a long talk with you, and there aren't any problems that can't be solved. Also that maybe I should come up myself for a weekend when I'm feeling better. Would that be a good idea? If it would, I will be recovered by a week from Friday and will arrive on the same flight Hymie took last weekend. Except I don't want to stay at that hotel you put Hymie in. He says the walls lean over the lobby and it doesn't sound safe to me. Also that there are birds and trees and a river yet in the lobby. Is it a hotel, or a national campground?

I remember you once told me the YMCA is as good as the Jack Tar, which I find hard to believe, but if you say so, I'll try it. After what Hymie spent at that bird farm last weekend, we can use the money I'll save at the Y. Do they take Jews?

I talked to Rachel Pomerantz's son the doctor last week, and he said there's nothing wrong with me but nerves, and what was wrong?

What could I tell him?

That my nephew Solly that I raised like my own son is queer? That would be great—he'd go home and tell his roommate, and what he tells his roommate, his roommate tells all his customers.

You know how women talk at the beauty parlor.

I wish young Dr. Pomerantz would get married, but Rachel says he's just not the marrying kind. Maybe if I introduced him to some nice girl (Linda Goldberg?) he'd be interested, since you apparently aren't.

Let me know if I should come up, and also what happened with you and Hymie last weekend.

Love,
Aunt Sylvia

P.S. Did Hymie remember to give you the recipe I sent up? It was for hot chopped pickle and peanut butter hors d'oeuvres. I'm sure your friends would have loved them if you used the recipe.—A.S.

There didn't seem to be any way out of it, so I sent Aunt Sylvia a brief accounting of the weekend, leaving out the worst parts, like the party, and what happened afterward. I should have known it wouldn't help. This time the letter got to me overnight.

Dear Solomon, [Back in trouble again!]

As you can see, I am writing this from the hospital where I went after I read your last letter. I can't believe you actually took your Uncle Hymie to those places. I went to him and asked him about it, and sure enough, he told me you actually took him to those places, and here I am. Young Dr. Pomerantz still says it's only nerves, but nerves don't make you get a fever, throw up, and break out in hives I won't tell you where. Still, maybe there's something to what Doctor says, and he says what's bothering me I should stop. So I should stop my only nephew from writing to me?

I'd die first.

But couldn't you now and then tell me something I could share with the mah-jongg ladies on Tuesday afternoons? You used to write me such nice letters about all the girls you were dating— I suppose none of it was true. Well, I mustn't let it worry me. Hymie says he doesn't think the life you're living is so bad, but I keep thinking about the things I've read, and I don't want you to have to call from the hospital sometime after you've had God-knows-what removed from your you-know-what. Tell me at least that you don't do what you do. It's not much, I know, but it would make me happy.

As for Sam Levitz, I've told Hymie that he's not to have that man in the house again, and I don't know what I'll say to poor Miriam. Last time I talked to her she said she thought Sam was going through the change. Such a change as Sam's gone through shouldn't happen to your father, and you know what I thought of your father may he rest in peace.

I have all your letters here with me in the hospital (the drawer in the bedstand has a lock, thank God—you know how nurses are) and I've been rereading them between tranquilizers. From what you have said, you don't seem to feel the way you ought to feel. A little guilt never hurt anyone, as I'll be the first to tell you. Hymie says it's none of my business, and it's your life to live any way you want, but if you ask your Aunt Sylvia, I think you ought to find a nice girl and settle down. What can there be in life without children and a nice home? I don't know what would have happened to me, childless as I was, if your father (may he rest in peace) hadn't done what he did to my sister (may she rest in peace). Not that I'm glad it happened, but Sadie never was much of a mother—she never should have had a child in the first place.

I'd better not try to write any more—they're coming in to give me an enema. They think maybe they can drain the worry from an aunt's heart that way?

Please, in your next letter don't tell me anything I don't want to know.

Tell me instead about the party.

Love,
Aunt Sylvia

Well, you have to admit, she *did* ask. And after a lot of soul searching, and a long talk with Scotty, who pointed out that she was already in the hospital and what more could happen, I told her about the party. Again, I left out the worst parts (never accuse me of having no feeling for my aunt), but apparently the parts I left in were enough. Back came another of her letters, three pages this time, written on both sides . . .

Solomon Steinberg! [Oh, boy, am I in it now!]

Suing? What is this with suing? Hymie is suing the police department? What is this with false arrest? They arrested my Hymie? For what? For vagrant? What is this with vagrant? My Hymie has never been vagrant in his life! I love you, Solomon, but if you are making all this up, I don't know what will happen. Are you for some reason trying to kill me? Well let me tell you—if that's what you're trying to do, it's working.

Food I don't eat.

Sleep I don't get.

Always, night and day, my stomach hurts. And the pain in my heart I won't burden you with. By next week Intensive Care is where I'll be, and I don't have to tell you about Intensive Care. *It's where they put you to die!!*

I talked to Hymie but all he said was not to worry. Not to worry! How can I not worry when I don't even know what not to worry about?

What can I tell Doctor?

He wants to know what's wrong. What do I tell him? My nephew the queer got my husband his uncle arrested for vagrant? It sounds like a disease nice people don't talk about.

I'm going to ring for the nurse and see if I can get something to sleep by. Maybe when I wake up, if I'm not dead I'll write some more.

So I'm not dead, and I got some sleep, and maybe I'm not going to die after all. Who has time to die, I ask you? What, I ask you, Solomon, would you do without me? Not to mention your Uncle Hymie for whom I am going to have to be a tower of strength in his moment of need though God alone knows where my strength will come from. Hymie is bringing some chicken soup when he comes to visit today, so that should help.

Solomon, I don't like to have to mention this, but I'm afraid you take after your father (may he rest in peace). There are things, Solomon, that I don't have to know. There is such a thing, Solomon, as too much truth. Truth is like candy—too much of it can make you sick. Which is probably why I'm in the hospital, now that I think of it.

Your father (R.I.P.) was always telling the truth to your mother (R.I.P.), and believe me, there were times when she didn't want to know. Like the time your father told your mother he was having an affair with her sister (not me—the one we

[77]

never talk about and now you know why). Now why did he do that? Who knows? Maybe he wanted to hurt her. Maybe he wanted to get it off his chest. Maybe he wanted her to forgive him.

Whatever.

But he didn't need to do it.

So he had an affair with his wife's sister. That should have been between them and God (who wouldn't have liked it) but he had to go spread it all over the family and make everybody unhappy. Of course, he didn't exactly do the spreading— your mother did that—but the result was the same: more truth than anybody needed to know. So what happened? You don't need to know— that's not what we're talking about. What we're talking about is you, and how you seem to be like your father.

All right, so you're queer, or gay, or whatever you want to call it. Why do I have to know all about it? You think I enjoy knowing about all this? Too much truth, that's what you're telling me. And look where it's got me.

In the hospital, that's where.

So tell me more about Hymie and the police. That I do need to know. And don't leave anything out—I'm already as sick as I'm going to get, so tell the truth. *About Hymie!* You, I don't want to hear about.

Love,
Aunt Sylvia

P.S. I'm going home Tuesday. With the world falling apart, who can be in the hospital?—A.S.

Truth is like candy? What does she mean, too much can make you sick? I always thought the truth was supposed to make you free, not sick. So maybe for her, free and sick are the same thing.

Well, not for me. And not for Uncle Hymie, either. He came up here to find out some truth, and did he get sick? No.

He got busted.

Actually, it wasn't really as bad as it sounds, unless you were in Uncle Hymie's position. All the rest of us at the party simply produced our identification, proved we were more or less what you could call up-standing citizens (we pay our parking tickets before they issue warrants), and that was that.

Except for Uncle Hymie.

You remember how Uncle Hymie was dressed, in the tight pants and the fishnet shirt? Well, one thing about those pants—they don't have pockets. So Uncle Hymie, not wanting to carry a purse, hadn't brought his wallet with him. After all, how was he to know Rita-Rose was going to get mad and call the cops? He didn't even *know* Rita-Rose. There he was, dressed like an overage hustler, and with no I.D. Did they believe him when he told them he was my Uncle Hymie visiting from Los Angeles?

Not hardly.

They muttered something about him being every-body's old auntie, and arrested him for being a va-grant. That means they weren't sure who he was, and he didn't have any money on him. They took him off to the city hotel on Bryant Street, where it's easy to check in but not so easy to check out. Also, the service isn't quite up to standard. Like, breakfast at seven is mandatory, and they make sure you're awake by rattling the bars.

When the cops took Uncle Hymie off to Bryant Street, everyone else just took off, no doubt to spread the word around town that I'd been raided, and ruin me socially for at least a week. (That can happen, you know—when you're hot, you're hot, and nobody wants to get burned. Except Uncle Hymie, who has already been burned, and is now in the cooler.)

The intricacies of extracting those near and dear to you from the clutches of the law are not easy to master, but that night I learned a lot. What you do is, you buy their freedom. If you can afford it.

Scotty and I figured the tab on Uncle Hymie wouldn't be too steep ($600 is par for the course, but at least Hymie had his pants on). We checked the cash supplies. Ten dollars between us, which will get you through about three drinks without too much left to lose if you should happen to get rolled.

Not, however, enough to get Uncle Hymie out.

While I hiked down to the corner bar to cash a check, Scott called a bondsman. The bondsman checked things out and estimated that fifty bucks on the barrelhead should spring Hymie. We went down to Bryant Street to play the waiting game.

The bondsman had found out that the cops weren't through with Uncle Hymie yet (it seems you can't get checked out until you're checked in), so we went down to the Raunch Room to have a beer.

And there sits Sam Levitz, all dolled up in his leather drag.

"No Hymie tonight?" he wanted to know.

"He's on Bryant Street," Scott said without thinking.

"There's nothing on Bryant Street but the jail."

I nodded. "That's where Uncle Hymie is."

Sam blinked.

"Hymie? In jail? You gotta be kidding me."

I told him what had happened, and one thing I'll say for Sam Levitz, the first thing he wanted to know was if we had enough money for the bail. We told him we had enough for a bond.

"A bond? Are you kidding? With a bond you lose the deposit. Post the cash yourself."

"We don't have the cash."

"So I got some. Come on, let's go get Hymie."

"Let's have another beer first," Scott said. "I'll cancel the bondsman, and there's no rush anyway. They haven't finished booking him yet."

I ordered the beers—Scotty's spent enough time bailing friends out of the slammer that he should know what he's talking about.

"For what are they booking him?" Sam wanted to know when I'd gotten the beers. "Don't tell me Hymie got caught at Grace Cathedral? Who'd believe it? He's not even Episcopalian."

I did my best to explain the whole thing to Sam, who mainly seemed to be interested in getting an introduction to Rita-Rose, and by the time I got done, it was about time to go to jail. We were lucky they didn't bust us, too, all things considered. I mean, there we were, me in my blazing gold caftan, Scott in a simple little jumpsuit with about twelve hundred buttons running up and down the seams, and Sam Levitz with his stomach hanging over a belt that looked like he'd stolen it off a dangerous dog. Also, tonight he's wearing a fishnet shirt under his leather jacket (it's cold), so he has the same tufted look that Uncle Hymie is sporting.

The desk sergeant peered at us.

Long silence.

"People like you don't usually come in here without the arresting officer," he sneered.

"People like us go where we want," Sam snarled right back. "Where's Hymie Leiberman?"

"You want to bail him?"

"That's right."

"You'll find a bondsman across the street."

"No bonds. Cash. How much?"

The sergeant picked up a phone, and made some mutterings. "One hundred dollars."

Sam produced the money, and the sergeant started filling out some papers. We spent the next couple of hours carrying papers around, getting this signed and that stamped, and were finally told to take the elevator to the sixth floor, which is where they had stashed Hymie and all the other drunks and desperados.

When the door opens on the sixth floor, you know you're in a jail. I mean, *you're* in the jail. They have a cage around the door to the elevator, and you have to call a guard, push the papers through the screen, then stand there like a chimpanzee while they go get you your criminal. Naturally, since it's a visitor's cage, it's small, and you're all squooshed up with an assortment of crying mothers, sullen wives, outraged lovers who are going to want to know just how it happened that Lance (or Troy) got picked up at the baths when he was supposed to be working late. (Outraged Lover, of course, isn't going to mention that the only reason he isn't in the slammer, too, is that he'd recognized Lance's (or Troy's) voice from the next room at that same baths, and decided that getting the hell out was the better part of valor.)

Pretty soon here comes Uncle Hymie, and I can tell he's mad. I mean, he's saying things to the officer with him that I won't repeat. The officer is taking it stoically. Apparently he's heard it before. As he pushes Hymie into the cage, he says, "If I were you, I'd take him home and give him a drink. He's stone sober, but he's damned mad. At his age, that can cause a heart attack."

"Don't 'heart attack' me!" Hymie yells. "When my lawyers finish with you, you'll be the one with the heart attack."

I could tell he was building up to a good scene, but fortunately the elevator arrived. We shoved him in just in time for him to hear the cop muttering something about "that's what all you fairies say," then the door slid shut. He spun around to yell something. That's when he first noticed Sam.

"Jesus, Sam, did they get you, too?"

"He bailed you out, Uncle Hymie," I said.

"Him? You, Sam? What'd you do that for? How'd you know I was here?"

"Solly and Scott were going to have a bond posted. I ran into them down the street, and knowing you, I figured we'd better put up the cash. So you owe me a hundred dollars, which you can pay me this morning if you have it. It was supposed to last me through till Monday, but I hadn't counted on bailing you out. I can cash a check, but then I'd have to explain it to Miriam, and that could get a little awkward."

"Sam, don't worry about the money. Where can we get a drink?"

"Home," I said.

"Sam? You'll come with us?"

"At four o'clock in the morning, where should I go?

Besides, unless you have the hundred now, I can't even afford a hustler."

Uncle Hymie's eyes popped.

"A hundred dollars for a hustler?"

"How much do you pay for a good hooker?" Sam countered.

I was starting to like Sam Levitz more and more.

13

Well, after I wrote to Aunt Sylvia, telling her as little as humanly possible about Uncle Hymie's bust, the letters fairly flew. Naturally, the first precinct heard from was Aunt Sylvia.

Dear Solly, [She must be mad at someone else now!]

What you wrote me I couldn't believe, so I showed your letter to Hymie. Is this true? I asked him. Substantially correct, he told me. What is substantially correct? I asked him. I want to know if all this really happened!

So, don't get excited, he told me. You'll make yourself sick. (As if I wasn't sick already!)

Sick! I said. How can I get sick? The world is falling apart, and you think I have time to get sick? Did you pay that pervert the money you owe him?

What pervert? Hymie asked. What pervert, I'm wondering. How many perverts does he know? Sam Levitz, I told him, so he'd know who I meant.

Sam Levitz is not a pervert, he told me. Hah! I thought. What does he know. But knowing how Hymie reacts when I say Hah, I didn't say it. Then he tells me that being different is not necessarily being perverted, so I asked him what he would call Sam Levitz.

A homosexual with masochistic tendencies, he tells me. Then he tells me that you would probably call him a leather queen, whatever that means.

He's a pervert, I told Hymie. You know what your uncle said to me then? He told me that Sam Levitz was responsible for him, whatever that means, and that I should keep a civil tongue in my head when he comes over.

He's not coming into my house, I said.

You have a house? Hymie asked me. Naturally I stared at him like he must of just had a stroke, because what else would make him say a thing like that? *This* house, I said, since obviously his stroke had made him forget. Hymie then lost whatever reality he ever had, because what he said next I couldn't believe.

This house, he said, is *our* house, what *I* paid for with the sweat of my brow, and Sam Levitz is welcome here any time he wants to come.

Are you defending him? I asked.

He bailed me out of jail, Hymie said. Where were you, he asked, when Sam was getting me out of jail?

Sometimes, Solly, I don't think your Uncle Hymie thinks too clearly. He seemed to think the whole thing was my fault. Did I ask him to go to all those places? Did I ask him to buy those strange clothes? Did I ask him to go to your party?

No!

All I asked him to do was go to San Francisco and get you straightened out. So now I'm going to have to come up there and do it myself. Not only you, but now I have to fix the mess Hymie's got himself into.

What I want you should do is this. I want you should get a psychiatrist and a lawyer. The psychiatrist is for you, the lawyer is for Hymie. You must know someone up there who could recommend someone in San Francisco. As for the lawyer, I'm told Melvin Belli is pretty good. Does he cost much?

If you can do that, I'll take care of everything else when I get there. I'll arrive on Friday, on the same flight as Uncle Hymie was on. Pick me up at the airport. I'm going to stay at your house—we'll need every cent we can lay our hands on. *And tell your friends to stay away.*

Love,
Aunt Sylvia

Now I knew who Aunt Sylvia was mad at, and since he was in trouble anyway, I turned to Uncle Hymie for help. I sent him Aunt Sylvia's letter, and asked him what to do.

Dear Solly,

You're asking me what to do? For forty years I've lived with your Aunt Sylvia and not known what to do. So how can I help you?

So I'll try.

First, there is no way to stop her from coming up there. Unless you come down here, should which happen, your Aunt Sylvia will have a team of doctors waiting to grab you. You want that? About like I wanted those cops to grab me at the party. So stay where you are, and get hold of a psychiatrist and a lawyer. But not just *any* shrink and shylock! For the lawyer, there's a man named Ben Jergens. Sam Levitz knows him (don't tell Sylvia) and says he's used to the kind of case we got, if you know what I mean. For the psychiatrist, don't you know anybody up there except decorators and hairdressers? Somebody sympathetic? Never mind—I'll talk to Sylvia's doctor. He should know someone up there, and I have a feeling if I explain the situation he'll be able to suggest something.

In the meantime, don't worry; I'll try to calm Sylvia down (as if she's ever been calm in her life) before she leaves. As for your friends—don't worry about that, either: she couldn't tell the gay ones from the straight ones without a label.

All I can tell you is this. She'll make a lot of noise, and stir things up as best she can, then, when the dust settles, she'll declare that everything's fine, and come home. It won't matter how things come out, just so she thinks she accomplished something.

Be glad Sylvia's only your aunt, Solly. As an aunt she can throw a scene and tear things up a little. But a good Jewish mother can throw a suicide. Fortunately for you, that can only happen once, so you're safe.

Love,
Uncle Hymie

Sure enough, a couple of days later there comes a classy cream-colored envelope from Mrs. Pomerantz's son-the-doctor:

Dear Mr. Steinberg,

Your uncle, Hymie Leiberman, has just left my office, and after discussing the whole situation with him, I think I can give you the name of the man you want to see. Contact Dr. James Coleman in the 450 Sutter Medical Building. He's a psychiatrist, and once you explain what's going on, I'm sure he can help you out. He was my lover in medical school, so you can see there's no problem there.

If your Aunt Sylvia had only told me in the first place what her problem was, I probably could have gotten her calmed down without all the fuss and bother. Apparently, though, from what your uncle said, Sylvia still thinks all of us wear tight pants and fluffy sweaters. (After my own mother met Bill, my lover, she asked me why I wanted to live with a queer. Naturally, it never occurred to her that *I* was one, too. So I told her. She didn't like it, but she's gotten used to it. In fact, she's come to appreciate Bill a lot. It seems he criticizes me almost as much as she does.)

Jimmy Coleman should be able to take Sylvia in hand. He's a very butch number, and he'll explain things to her in a way that, while it might not satisfy her fondest dreams (i.e., that you should get married and have six kids), will at least get her off your back. I can't speak for him, of course, but he'll probably give her the old "incurable disease" line. He doesn't believe it, but he finds families are often more ready to accept a terminal illness than an alternate life-style. Straight people are weird. But then, you already knew that, didn't you?

Hoping everything will turn out all right, I am,

Sincerely yours,
Marvin Pomerantz, M.D.

The name Jimmy Coleman rang a big gong in my mind. I went searching through all my old trick sheets, and sure enough, I had his phone number. It seems I'd met him in a bar a few months earlier, and we'd swapped phone numbers. He'd never called me, though, and I hadn't called him. (That's how those things usually go—everybody's waiting for someone else to make the first move.)

It seemed a little odd, calling a trick-who-never-was to make a professional appointment, but what the hell. So I procrastinated, then dashed off a note to Aunt Sylvia, telling her I didn't really think her trip was necessary, but if she was going to insist on coming anyway, at least I'd line her up with a team of professionals.

I also told her to forget Melvin Belli—I didn't think she'd be interested, once she found out his prices, and I didn't really see Belli spending a lot of time on Uncle Hymie, either.

I finished up by letting her know that she should postpone her trip till Monday (since I'd planned a nice weekend) and let her know that she shouldn't count on me being at her beck and call all the next week, either. I'd made the appointments, but I was damned if I was going to trot all over town with her. I can trot all over town on my own, if I want to. After telling her that I thought she should let Hymie handle his case, and let me handle my life, I signed off.

The reply came like a speeding bullet.

Dear Solomon, [Uh-oh!]

I did not like the tone of your last letter, but if you're as busy as you say you are you probably did not realize that you were not showing the proper respect for the woman who raised you. So I'll overlook it, as I've had to overlook so many things in my life.

That you should go out of town for the weekend when you knew I'm planning to come up to you I can't understand. It seems to me that you should show more concern, if not for me, then for yourself and your uncle. After all, Solly, all I'm trying to do is help. All I want is that you should have a full and happy life.

All I want is what's best for you.

All I want is that you should get married. To a woman!

But of course, what I want is not important, is it? It's more important that you should give yourself over to the sinful pleasures of your illness, isn't it? Well, enjoy! But remember, the time will come when I'll be gone, and you won't be able to thank me for all I've done for you and all I'm still going to do for you. I do not ask for your thanks, Solly, for what I'm doing is an act of unselfish love. Maybe someday, should my prayers be answered, you'll understand that.

Maybe also someday I'll see Jerusalem.

So I will not ask you to give up two days of your precious time for your aunt who raised you. Instead, I will do as you ask, and wait until Monday. In the meantime, while you are indulging yourself try to remember that you are ruining your Uncle Hymie's life. I know that what you are doing to me does not matter to you, but try to have some regard for your uncle. After all, without him, where would you be now? Without *you,* he would not have a prison sentence hanging over his head.

Think about *that,* Solomon!

Love always,
Aunt Sylvia

_____

Why did I ever tell her I was gay in the first place? All I was getting for my trouble was another dose of guilt. Now I was supposed to feel badly about myself, her, and Uncle Hymie, too!

It was as if I'd committed a cardinal sin.

Well, let's face it—I did. I didn't turn out to be the nice little Jewish boy she wanted. So couldn't she have wanted a nice little Jewish faggot?

But nobody wants that.

Nobody wanted Solly Steinberg, either, including Murray Roberts. When I swapped off Solly for Murray, too bad I couldn't have turned in the family for a bunch of Methodists. Or, even better, Unitarians.

The next day I talked to Jimmy Coleman. He'd gotten a note from Marvin Pomerantz, so it wasn't like he wasn't expecting my call. I didn't tell him I'm actually Murray Roberts—he probably doesn't remember me (if he does, why didn't he call?); and besides, I'd rather surprise him. I made an appointment, hoping he doesn't charge too much, and wondering if maybe he'd be willing to take his fee out in trade.

On the other hand, maybe I'd rather pay him. Then again, I *did* take his phone number, so he couldn't be too bad, unless I was drunk, which I probably was.

Meanwhile, I had to figure out what to do with Aunt Sylvia, and I came to a decision.

Either she was going to have to accept me the way I was, or get out of my life!

I was damned if I was going to go on letting her call me a pervert, but I was also damned if I'd let her pretend I was anything but what I was. I mean, you'd think she'd realize that her way of life isn't the only way. God knows, people like her have been making sure for years that people like me don't think we're perfect. So, is she? On the other hand, she hadn't hit town yet, so it was safe to make such resolutions as I was making.

The resolutions firmly in place, I went off to have dinner with Scott, who was dying to know what was going on. I thought about telling him that Uncle Hymie had run off with Sam Levitz, and Aunt Sylvia had entered a convent, but he'd never have believed it—he knows Uncle Hymie isn't Sam Levitz's type.

14

I went to see Jimmy Coleman a couple of days later, and remembered why I hadn't called him.

I didn't have the courage.

Jimmy Coleman is six-foot-three, with dark wavy hair, and the most gorgeous blue eyes I've ever seen. The minute I walked into his office, I remembered him. I met him in a bar one night, and drank myself silly trying to get up the guts to ask him for a date. All I got was his phone number and a hangover, and by the time I was over the hangover, I was too chicken to use the phone number.

When I walked in there that day, he looked at me (which destroyed me) and said, "I know you, don't I?"

I owned up. He remembered the incident.

"Too bad you didn't use your real name," he said. "I have a thing for Jewish boys."

Aha! I thought. It's never too late. For the first time in weeks, things were looking up.

Anyway, I filled him in on the situation, and we more or less agreed on a plan of attack. He'd see Aunt

Sylvia, and go through a lot of clucking and hair-pulling over the tragedy that has befallen her. Also, he'd agree that I needed help (which I did—I needed all the help I could get in getting Jimmy Coleman into bed!) but that he'd have to know a lot more about me before he could undertake to straighten me out. Will she be willing to come in and talk about me? If she won't, fine! But if she will, well, all I can say is watch out, Aunt Sylvia—you may think it's my head that's getting shrunk, but it's really going to be yours!

Monday afternoon, I picked Aunt Sylvia up at the airport. Considering she'd been feeling rotten for months, and spent two weeks in the hospital, she looked great. Good color, a glint in her eye that scared the hell out of me, and the fighting spirit that only an embattled Jewish mother can muster.

All the way into the city she assured me that everything was going to be all right, that she didn't hold anything against me, that the mess that was my life wasn't my fault, that my illness could be cured, and that her love would conquer all.

In short, it looked like it was going to be a terrible week.

I got her stowed away in the guest room, and while she was unpacking, I called Scott to arrange for him to phone me around ten thirty that night with an emergency. I had a feeling I was going to need a drink, and since Aunt Sylvia didn't approve of my drinking any more than she approved of my love life, I figured I'd need an excuse to get out of the house.

I was right.

While I was fixing dinner, Aunt Sylvia busied herself with some minor redecorating, primarily involving turning my statue of David to the wall. Needless to say, it has no more fig leaf on the back than on the front, and Michelangelo must have been an ass man. David reversed is much more suggestive than David straight on.

Dinner was fairly calm, but afterward Aunt Sylvia announced that it was time for us to have A Talk.

I grew up with her. When she says we're going to have A Talk, that means *I'm* going to have A Listen. So I listened.

After an hour and a half of her heterosexual moralizations on the glories of procreation and parenthood (no mention of personal happiness or emotional satisfaction), the telephone mercifully rang, and Scott announced the requested emergency. I trotted down to the corner for my drink.

One was not enough.

By the time I got home, Aunt Sylvia had gone to bed, and the dogs were ready for their walk. About halfway down Polk Street I ran into a gorgeous Afghan, but his roommate was home, and I didn't want to risk waking Aunt Sylvia, so I took the dogs back home, and considered the wisdom of spending the night at the baths.

In the end, I decided to go to bed. I had the feeling I was going to need all my strength, since Aunt Sylvia was due for Round One with the doctor and the lawyer on Tuesday morning.

Also, something told me liquor consumption in San Francisco was going to take a sudden upturn that week.

Tuesday I spent the entire day with Mrs. Hale. She wanted to redo her entire dining room in sea green.

Not just sea green accents in a nice formal white dining room.

Oh, no.

What she wanted was the whole damned *thing* in sea green. With salt-water aquaria as accents. Can you imagine trying to eat vichyssoise with an octopus staring over your shoulder? Not to mention the smell. But if that's what she wanted, what did I care? God knows, she doesn't invite *me* to dinner. So I agreed to spend a few thousand of her husband's dollars on fishnet (maybe I can buy the fishnet used from Sam Levitz) and some tacky sea shells, drown the whole thing in plastic kelp, mark it all up four hundred percent, and make her happy.

That was my day, up to my ass in sea urchins. And what did I get when I got home? Did I get to sit down to a nice heart-to-heart bitch session with Scotty over four or five martinis? No. I got to sit down to a Cel-Ray tonic with Aunt Sylvia.

It's not that she didn't know I drank. It's just that she'd decided there were going to be some changes in my life. Not only did I have to be straight, I had to be sober. (I can just barely face straight people without a drink under my belt. Facing myself straight would require total alcoholism).

We sat down with our Cel-Ray tonics, and she told me about her day.

She, it seems, had met with the lawyer, and he'd treated her to a real war conference. Apparently he didn't bother to tell her that he'd already gotten the whole thing straightened out. Instead, he decided to have some fun, and told Aunt Sylvia that Uncle Hymie was guilty as hell—and not just of the charges as booked.

Aunt Sylvia said she set him straight in a hurry and I guess he let her think she'd convinced him that Hymie wasn't actually going down on any of the guests at the party. Then he launched into a Gay Rights speech, and tried to convince Aunt Sylvia that they should make a test case out of the whole thing, call in reporters, sue the city, and be prepared to dress Uncle Hymie up in his fishnet shirt and flare pants and drag him off to the Supreme Court. Aunt Sylvia did not buy it.

"My Hymie," as she put it, her voice filled with pain, "he wants to paint lavender and drag off to Washington."

Unfortunately, I snickered.

"You should laugh," she squalled at me, the accusatory finger leveled in the vicinity of my nose. "It's not your reputation that shyster wants to ruin. Should you have a reputation left, God pity your soul!"

I assured her that I had a reputation, of sorts, and that she shouldn't worry about it. Then I fixed myself a gin and Cel-Ray tonic, which, I can tell you, is not nearly as bad as it sounds.

So after assuring the lawyer that all she wanted was for him to get the charges dismissed ("and double the price if you can keep it out of the newspapers!"), Aunt Sylvia went to see Dr. Coleman.

"Such a nice man," she said about the good doctor.
(I agreed, but not out loud.)
"So understanding of the problem."
(Tell me!)
"He seems to think he can fix you."
(Hunh?)
"But it'll take a while."
(I hope so—like maybe the rest of my life?)

"So you're going to see him tomorrow."

"Tomorrow?" Now I was speaking out loud.

"Tomorrow."

"Aunt Sylvia, I have to work tomorrow."

"So what do you have to do that's more important than that you should straighten out your life?"

"I have a long meeting with Mrs.—"

"Mrs. Whoever-she-is can wait. What's so important about her sofas? They're threadbare maybe?"

"Well, no . . ."

"Well, nothing. You'll go to see Dr. Coleman at eleven sharp. And you shouldn't be late: he says he doesn't like to be kept waiting."

"I'll bet," I muttered.

"What?"

"I said I'll bet he doesn't like to be kept waiting. And I'll bet damned few people have ever *kept* him waiting."

"What's that supposed to mean?"

"Nothing. When do you see him again?"

"You at eleven. Me at two."

I was beginning to see the light. Dr. Coleman wanted me in for a strategy meeting. Fine—I was for that.

Well, you can imagine how the evening went. We kept on sparring, or at least Aunt Sylvia sparred, while I ducked.

Mitzie and Fritzie had the good sense to stay out of the whole fracas until it came time for them to go potty. Then they joined the party, doing their usual relay race between me and the front door. It took a while before Aunt Sylvia noticed them, and they caught her in midsermon.

"I don't know about those dogs, Solly," she said.

"They look like they should belong to a hairdresser."

"They did," I said, heading for the door. "I fucked him out of them." I opened the door. "Literally," I said. Then I closed the door behind me.

I don't know exactly why I said that.

I wish I could report that Aunt Sylvia was in bed when I got back, but I can't.

"What did that mean?" she demanded upon my return. It was as if I had never been gone.

"You really want to know?" I asked.

"No," she replied. "But I want you should tell me anyway."

I fixed myself a drink.

A real one.

Then I sat down and faced Aunt Sylvia. There was one of those long silences wherein the Jewish aunt tries to forestall the conversation she has demanded. The nephew tries to weigh his chances of coming out of the conversation without getting a free nose job. I took the plunge.

"I was dating a hairdresser. He had a poodle. The poodle had puppies. Are you following, so far?"

Aunt Sylvia nodded. She did not speak, but she nodded.

"All right. So one night we were at his place, and I decided I wanted to ball him. You know 'ball'?"

Again, Aunt Sylvia nodded, but her silence got louder.

"All right. So I made the suggestion that I should ball him, and he said no, because it would hurt. So we made a bet. If it hurt, I took him out to dinner. If it didn't hurt, I got one of the puppies."

"So that only accounts for one of the dogs," Aunt

Sylvia said, ducking the main thrust of the story. I shrugged.

"The next night we had a rematch. I probably would have wound up with the whole litter if he hadn't decided it was a losing proposition."

There was a long silence while Aunt Sylvia turned things over in her mind, which was better than I had expected. I had more or less thought she'd start turning things over in my house.

"You really did that?" she said at last.

I nodded.

"It's sick."

"It isn't," I replied. "For one thing, the guy really wanted to try it. If he hadn't, he wouldn't have made the bet in the first place. Besides, if it had hurt, I wouldn't have done it, and would have cheerfully taken him out to dinner."

"So how did you know it wouldn't hurt?" (Aunt Sylvia has a talent for the irrelevant.)

"I didn't. But I was pretty sure. For one thing, he was relaxed, because he knew I wouldn't do anything to him he didn't want me to do. We're not rapists, despite what you may have heard. For another thing, if it'll make you feel any better, you can rest easy knowing that your nephew is not exactly what you could call a disaster in the bedroom. Any other questions?"

I have to hand it to Aunt Sylvia. She didn't fly off into a rage, and she didn't scream "pervert." Instead, she simply smashed her glass in the fireplace and stomped off to bed.

Tuesday was a disaster from beginning to end, and when I got home, I discovered that Aunt Sylvia had decided to wash the dogs. Well, I mean, they looked *ghastly*, and they knew it. Mitzie was hiding under a chair, and Fritzie wouldn't come out of the bathroom, and Aunt Sylvia wouldn't stop looking smug. Fortunately, I caught Peter, from the poodle parlor, just before he left for the night, and he came right over and picked them up. God knew what he could do with them—their coats were simply wrinkled beyond belief—but he said a few lanolin treatments and a lot of brushing would put them right back in shape. It cost me a couple of hundred dollars, but at least they knew who they were again. When I got home, they'd looked like they lived in Daly City with five brats grabbing at them all day. It was not the perfect ending to a perfect day.

In fact, it was simply the cap to an otherwise lousy day. First there was Mrs. Hale again. She thought my idea of garlanding the dining room with plastic kelp was perfect, and was wondering how much it would cost to have about five hundred yards of the stuff made up. God help me!

Needless to say, by eleven I was ready for a session with Jimmy Coleman. I'd thought maybe lunch.

"Sit down," he said when I came in. I suppose I looked forty: God knows I *felt* sixty.

"Let's have a couple of drinks and lunch," I said. "This afternoon's going to be a real double-edged bitch."

"Sit down," he repeated. "You have a problem."

"I do?"

"Your Aunt Sylvia."

"Oh, no," I said. "She's your problem, remember? All you have to do is convince her that I'm normal."

He leaned back and lit a cigarette.

"If you grew up with her, I find it hard to believe that you could be normal," he drawled.

I sat down.

"Don't be ridiculous," I said. "Of course I'm normal."

"How old are you?"

"Twenty-eight."

"How old?" (His brows sort of arched.)

"All right, I'm thirty-four. What's wrong with that?"

"Nothing. Thirty-four is a perfectly good age. Why do you want to be twenty-eight?"

"Mainly because when I'm forty-four, I'll want to be thirty-eight, and I believe in getting an early start," I said a bit testily. "Now, how about lunch?"

"I don't eat lunch."

I begin to understand why he has such a trim figure.

"Well, I do," I grumped. "Now, what's going on with Aunt Sylvia?"

Coleman leaned back and put his hands behind his head, which made his chest fill out, which made my heart flutter.

"Not much," he replied. "She's convinced that 'queers,' as she calls us, are sick, and she's also convinced that you're miserable. Are you?"

"I wasn't, but if she stays around very long, I will be." (I was beginning to get sour.)

"You really don't like her very much, do you?"

"What do you mean?" (When in doubt, counter.)

He just sat there looking at me, and after a while I began to feel guilty, which I suppose is a reflex action with me. But finally I decided I'd better say something.

"I just want her to stop bitching at me about getting married," I offered.

"What's wrong with being married?" (He can counter, too.)

"To a *girl?*" (Got him on that one!)

"You didn't mention the gender involved." (Got me right back, damn it!)

"Well, that's what I meant."

"Are you sure?"

"Oh, for shit's sake," I said, getting just a tad exasperated. "I've *been* married. Three times."

"Thus do people refer to the instability of gay relationships."

"They were all bastards," I said as piously as possible.

"You married them," Coleman pointed out. God, I hate reasonable people!

"I also divorced them."

"Why did you marry them?"

"The first one I was in love with. The second one was great in bed. The third one was a nice guy."

"What happened to him?" (*He's* getting awfully snoopy.)

"He left me."

"He left you?" (Do I hear a note of incredulity?)

"Oh, he came back. But I figured if he did it once he'd do it again, so I walked out on him."

"How terribly adult of you." (The damned brow arched again.)

"What's that supposed to mean?"

"Well, since you're not my patient, I suppose I can explain a few things to you."

"You don't explain things to your patients?" (What the hell kind of shrink is this?)

"Never," he said, treating me to a smile designed to floodlight the Transamerica Building, which is several blocks away. "If I solve their problems for them, they blame me every time something goes wrong in their lives."

Perhaps there was a key to Aunt Sylvia here, but I didn't say anything. I just listened. He kept talking (and he's a baritone, which is easy on the ears).

"I make them work things out for themselves. That way they only face things they're ready to face, and their decisions are their own. So if they fuck up, it's their own damn fault."

"Sort of takes you off the hook, doesn't it?" I pointed out.

He smiled his smile again. "I try never to get on the hook in the first place."

"Clever you," said clever me, hoping to sound barbed. He ignored it, however, and leaned further back in his chair, blew a smoke ring, and gave me a look at his profile. My knees got weak.

"You know," he said. "It's people like you who give us a bad name."

"Hunh?" (There I go again with the bright riposte.)

"I saw some of your letters to your aunt. Do you really think she wants to know you pick people up off the street and ball them?"

"It happens. It's real." (Who does he think he is?)

"It happens. But how real is it?"

"Oh, please! It's part of gay life!"

"Part of growing up, maybe," he said. He sounded so sanctimonious I could have hit him, but instead I got sarcastic. You know something? It doesn't do you any more good to get sarcastic with a shrink than with an aunt.

"I'm thirty-four years old," I purred. "I really think I'm grown up."

"I'd be more inclined to put you in late adolescence," he said, thus blowing the old sarcastic act out of the water. Then, finally, he must have noticed that I was getting upset, because his feet came off the desk, and he leaned forward.

"Look," he said. "Gay people are different from straight people, right? We think differently, we act differently, we have different values, we have different interests. So where does it come from? Does it all just appear when we find out we're gay?"

"Well—" I began.

"Don't interrupt. If I listen, it costs you fifty dollars an hour. If I talk, it's free."

With that kind of money involved, I decided I'd better listen. I mean, I'm not even getting fifty an hour for filling Mrs. Hale's dining room with kelp!

He begins talking:

"All of us were brought up to be nice heterosexual American boys, with nice heterosexual American values and attitudes, right? But what happens? When we get to be about twenty or so, we find out we're not nice straight American boys. We're nice gay American boys. And all of a sudden we realize that everything we've been brought up to believe in doesn't fit. All our morals, so carefully stuffed into us since the crib, are designed to make the straight world orderly. But we don't live in the straight world."

At this point, he got up and began wandering around the room, looking very professorial, and I, who once had a crush on my Hebrew School teacher, was fascinated.

"For example," he said, lighting another cigarette, which I happen to think is very sexy. "All our lives we were taught that men going to bed with men is unnatural and immoral. Perverted. Then we find out that we *like* to go to bed with men—that for us, going to bed with women is unnatural. So we have a choice. Either accept the morals of our youth, and go directly into psychosis, or chuck the morals. Most of us, naturally, chuck the morals. . . ."

I was about to make one of my usual bright remarks, but I suddenly realized that Dr. Coleman was not kidding, and that maybe I should keep the bright remark to myself. So I shut up, lit a cigarette (which I hoped he would think was very sexy), and kept listening. And he kept talking. One thing about shrinks—give them a chance, and they can talk forever.

"The problem is that for most people, if you chuck one moral, you chuck them all. Toss the baby out with the bath, as it were. So then what do we have? We have a bunch of twenty-year-old infants with no idea of how they're supposed to behave, with no framework for their lives. For most gay people, it's sort of like being abandoned in infancy and left to fend for themselves with no help whatsoever. So, since nobody tells them how to behave, they behave any way they like at any given moment.

"When you consider everything, it's really kind of surprising that as many of us survive as do. If the straight people only knew what it's like to have to start growing up all over again just at the age when you thought you'd already done it—"

"Yes?" I said, since he seemed to have lost his voice.

"Oh, I was just thinking about a lot of my patients. The middle-aged women who think they have problems. God knows most of them have probably created more problems than they've ever had thrust on them.

Sometimes I feel like just telling them to shut the fuck up and go away."

"Why don't you?"

"I need their money. And they need me. Too bad more of the gay kids can't afford me. They really need the help, but most of them can't afford it and even the ones who can don't think they need it. And maybe they don't. All they really need is time to grow up. But it's hard, trying to grow up when the world assumes you already have."

"How would you like to have dinner some night?" I suggested, hoping to break what was fast becoming a morbid conversation. "Maybe we could discuss your middle-aged adolescence."

"It's yours we're worried about," Coleman pointed out. "However, if we have dinner, you have to promise not to let me talk shop. We'll go dancing, or something."

Now that was more like it. From the dance floor to the bedroom is a much easier step than from the couch to the floor. So I confirmed the date for Saturday night, sent a prayer up to whoever might be listening, begging Him to get Aunt Sylvia out of town by the weekend, and made my way back to the traumas of Jackson Square and the fabric shops.

I'm in the wrong business—Jimmy Coleman gets fifty dollars an hour just to listen to boring women. I only get forty, and I have to hang their curtains!

Well, so much for the morning. The afternoon wasn't too bad, until I got home to Mitzie, Fritzie, and the washerwoman of Roxbury Drive.

Needless to say, Aunt Sylvia wanted to know all about my conference with the doctor. I told her we talked a lot about my youth, and perhaps something would work out. (Like maybe on Saturday night?)

Another day was shot, and I was left alone with my thoughts.

I kept wondering if maybe Jimmy Coleman was right, and I was trying to hurt Aunt Sylvia. All I really wanted was for her to accept me the way I was. And I wasn't really so bad.

I mean, Uncle Hymie didn't seem so upset about me, but then, nothing ever upsets Uncle Hymie. I decided I was sort of like him—nothing shocked me. Or maybe I was just shell-shocked.

I began thinking about some of the things I'd done, and I began to remember what I'd thought of them years earlier, before I'd done them. Like going to the baths.

The idea of the baths used to revolt me. All those people making it with each other; no conversation, no names, just sex. It's like going to a whorehouse, except you pay a flat fee at the door, and everybody's an amateur.

But on the other hand, there's a certain honesty about it: everybody's there for the same reason, and you don't have to pretend there's any emotion going on. (After three lovers, who needs emotion?) Also, you don't have to get drunk while you're trying to find out if the guy wants to make it with you: you simply grab him, and he either says yes or tells you that he's just resting. If he says he's just resting, there are fifty other people around, and one of them has to have some energy. So all it is, is advanced masturbation, and God and Kinsey know everybody masturbates.

I began to wonder what Jimmy Coleman thought of

the baths, and decided I should ask him on Saturday night. Then I decided maybe I shouldn't.

I didn't sleep too well Tuesday night.

I spent most of Wednesday in Jackson Square checking out the furniture and the faggots. There was a good-looking number in one of the fabric houses, but the old auntie that ran the place had an awfully proprietary look about her. God, I hope I never turn into one of those dismal old queens who buys boys. On the other hand, be nice to dirty old men: you'll be one yourself some day.

Aunt Sylvia had another session with Dr. Coleman, and was strangely silent at dinner. She kept eyeing me as if she was seeing me for the first time, then looking tragically at her peas. Toward the end of the meal she seemed to be working herself up to letting me in on the secret (not that I particularly wanted to know about it), but I managed to get off to my regular Wednesday night bridge game before she got started. I made a Bath Coup against Scotty—too bad he wasn't sober enough to realize it.

Then when I took Mitzie and Fritzie out for their walk, things started getting weird. What happened was, I got cruised, which is not so sensational in itself. What was strange was that when he finally got around to inviting me up for the standard cup of coffee, I didn't want to go. Instead, I said I couldn't, but how would he like to go to a movie next week? My God, he practically ran away. What, I wondered, had I done that was so wrong? All right, so it's not exactly street etiquette to try to make a date (almost as bad as asking for a last name), but was it really so terrible? What really scared me, though, was that I didn't know why

I did it. I began to have the feeling that something was brewing, and I wasn't at all sure I was going to like it.

When I got home, I called Scotty and made a date for lunch at the Gold Rush the next day. Also, I found a note from Aunt Sylvia, saying I had an appointment with Jimmy Coleman at two o'clock the next afternoon. (I thought one was supposed to make one's own appointments with the shrink, but then maybe one doesn't have an Aunt Sylvia. Maybe one is lucky.)

I was almost in a mood to call Uncle Hymie and have him call Aunt Sylvia home before my whole neatly structured world came crashing down around me, but I didn't suppose it would work. Aunt Sylvia is not usually happy till the temple lies in ruins at her feet.

As I dozed off, I came up with a wonderful idea. I decided to wear the gold lamé caftan to the breakfast table the next morning. That, I was sure, would brighten up the conversation.

15

Oh, boy, did it ever brighten the conversation.

Aunt Sylvia gazed at me over her coffee.

"Solly?" (More of a croak than her usual bellow.)

"Who else?" (I am acting like nothing is strange.)

"In a dress?"

"It's not a dress. It's a caftan."

"Don't tell me from caftan. It's a dress, and it looks like you stole it off a Miami hooker, forgive I should mention such a thing over breakfast."

"It's a caftan," I insisted. "And I didn't steal it from anybody. I had it made for me."

"That?" She was beginning to find her voice. "You had that made? You can afford to waste your money on things like that? What you need is—"

"A wife?" I said, keeping my voice as neutral as possible, which was not easy.

"All right, so that's probably not going to happen."

Well, I almost dropped my bagel. Was there really a glimmer of hope? "What led you to think that?" I asked, all innocence.

"Dr. Coleman. He doesn't seem to think he can cure you."

"He doesn't?" (Fancy that!)

"It seems there's two kinds of queers. Born queers and learned queers."

"And I'm born?" (Give her the rope, and she'll hang herself!)

"That's what Dr. Coleman thinks. Probably you get it from your father's side."

I'm afraid I may have stared at her just a little. This was a new twist. "From my father's side? What makes you think that?"

"Well, it couldn't have been your mother's side. That's *my* side. And there was always something strange about your father—"

"What?"

"The way he chased girls all the time. I always wondered, what's he trying to prove? It seemed a little . . ."

"Queer?" I offered.

Aunt Sylvia stared into her coffee cup, stirring madly. "Maybe I shouldn't use that word."

"It has a definite meaning as well as a connotative one," I offered.

"Whatever that means," Aunt Sylvia rejected.

"It means—"

"I don't need to know. I got enough to think about without you should clutter up my mind with fancy words. What were we talking about?"

"All kinds of things. It started with my caftan."

She stared at me for a long time. I pretended to read the newspaper. Try to pretend you're reading the newspaper when you know the bazookas are trained at you from point-blank range and may be fired at any moment.

"Solly," she began.

I looked up and braced myself.

"Actually, when you get used to it, and remember that it isn't a dress, what you got on isn't so bad. Very chick, really."

That, I suppose, was her idea of an olive branch.

"I understand they're very 'in' in Miami," I said by way of a conversation starter.

"On *all* the men?" (Some things are hard for Aunt Sylvia to grasp.)

"Not yet. We're usually a couple of years ahead of the straight crowd. But they'll catch on." I saw no point in telling her that caftans had been "out" for years. Why fall behind, just when you're getting ahead?

"Maybe I should get one for Hymie . . ."

"Not yet. Wait awhile, till you know if everybody's going to be wearing them."

"So why shouldn't Hymie be ahead of things?"

"Why should he?" That gave her pause.

"Of course, in Beverly Hills—" she began.

"Exactly," I said, pouncing. "Beverly Hills is not exactly Miami Beach or San Francisco."

"I'll bet I could find one, though," she said, perking right up.

I had a sudden vision of her dragging poor Uncle Hymie into Saks. They whip right up to some number with four rings on each hand and demand a caftan. His eyebrow arches (but not like Jimmy Coleman's) and he informs them that in the next block there is a branch of Omar the Tentmaker's. Aunt Sylvia spends the next two hours searching Rodeo Drive for an awning shop. Not a good idea.

"They only sell them south of Olympic," I said, knowing that Aunt Sylvia wouldn't hold with anything that was south of Olympic. There are, after all, limits to what one will do, even for Aunt Sylvia.

"Oh," she said, slumping a little. I could tell that she was sort of counting on the caftan to prove her liberality the way whites count on an occasional sparerib to prove theirs.

Aunt Sylvia pondered the loss of the caftan while I stuck "orts" and "ulpe" into the crossword puzzle.

"Maybe we should have lunch together today," she began.

"I'm meeting a friend of mine," I noncommittallized.

"The way you said that, Solly, it must be one of *those* friends."

My newspaper went down.

"If you mean a gay friend, yes, he is gay, and yes, he is a friend." (That set her back, let me tell you!)

"So don't get angry. It does bad things to the indigestion."

"I'm not angry. But please don't be sneery about my friends. Don't forget, I'm one of *those* people, too."

"How can I forget, with you shoving it down my throat all the time?"

"Maybe if you'd swallow it, I'd stop shoving it."

"Keep a civil tongue in your head, Solomon!"

Well, that tore it. I figured I was close enough to the goal to try for a forward charge, so I put the paper aside and faced her.

"Aunt Sylvia, I am a thirty-four-year-old man. I support myself very well. I live in a manner I choose to live in, and I have no intention of changing my life-style to suit you. As long as you are in my home, *you* will keep a civil tongue in *your* head, not vice versa. I'm more than glad to have you here, and as long as you're interested in finding out how I am, or what I am, great. But do not try to change me."

I didn't wait for an answer. I went upstairs, dressed, and left.

The morning did not go well. I suggested to one customer that she do her living room in pale blue to match her hair, and told another that parchment wallpaper in her bathroom would go well with her skin. Those two comments probably cost me about two grand each, but I didn't care. I got to the Gold Rush at eleven and was well into my third martini by the time Scotty arrived.

"My God, darling," he said, squeezing in next to me. "You look like you just fell off the cross."

"Jewish boys always look like that. Check my wrists for holes. Want a drink?"

"Don't I always? And believe me, I need one. I was only in bed for two hours last night, and that was in some horrible hotel on Sixth Street."

"Sixth Street," I repeated, choking on my olive. "What were you doing, chasing hustlers again?"

"Worse. I picked up a whore."

"Oh, Christ. What happened?"

"Who knows?" Scotty groaned, holding his head. "I was so drunk I didn't realize how ugly she was till this morning. I took her into the Kokpit last night."

"The troops must have loved that." I ordered him another drink.

"It was absolutely grotesque. They all kept telling me to get rid of her, so naturally I didn't. God only knows what I'll have to get rid of now."

"Don't tell me you screwed her?" This time I ordered *myself* another drink.

"Well, sort of," Scotty said, obviously doing his best to remember. "But she was so fat I'm not sure I ever got it in. All I know is I woke up this morning and there was this mass of tits all over the bed. I felt so butch I almost threw up."

"I may yet."

"Now, Murray, don't be that way."

"You know how I feel about women."

"All right. But fucking one now and then only makes you appreciate men more."

"Thanks anyway, but my appreciation is quite sufficient as it is. You must have been in great shape for work this morning."

"Like something the cat dragged in. Order me another drink. After this morning, I need it—someone told my boss I'd been at work drunk last week."

"Well, you were." And the week before, and the week before that!

"Well, of *course* I was, but nobody could tell. Besides, the bastard claimed I was drunk on Thursday, and that's the one day I was sober. Unfortunately, I've gotten to the point where people think I'm sober when I'm drunk, and vice versa. I suppose that's some kind of alcoholism, but I can't worry about it now. This morning was ghastly. I stopped for a quick one on the way to work, and then at ten I had to go in to see the boss. 'Harney,' he says, 'I have a report here that you were drunk last week.' Naturally, I denied it categorically."

"Naturally," I agreed. I mean, what else could he have done?

"So we had a little heart-to-heart, and I assured him

that I would *never* drink before coming to work—"

"Staying very far away from him, I trust."

"Well, of course. God, if he'd struck a match in front of my mouth, the whole room would have blown up."

"So did he believe you?"

"Naturally. I'm always very convincing with a couple of drinks under my belt. As soon as I got done talking to him, I ran across the street for a quick one to get me through till lunch."

He finished his drink and signaled Ivan for another.

"Next week," he said, draining half the fresh drink, "I've really *got* to go on the wagon."

"For you, that means no booze before lunch."

"*And* getting to bed by two in the morning," he added, a bit sanctimoniously.

"Your virtue overwhelms me." There was a moment of silence while Scotty cruised himself in the mirror over the bar.

"You know," he said after he'd winked back at himself, "we queens must be genetically different."

"Oh?"

"Well, look at us. Here we are, carrying on all the time, out drinking and screwing every night, and yet most of us look at least five years younger than straights our age."

"The glories of clean living, obviously," I observed.

"I'll drink to that," Scotty slurred. "Was Aunt Sylvia still up when you got home last night?"

"No, but she sure was this morning."

I filled him in on the grim details. He nodded soberly into his fourth (or fifth) drink.

"Well, at least she's starting to come around a little."

"Yeah, if I didn't wreck it by getting touchy."

"Well, we all get touchy now and then."

"But we don't all have an Aunt Sylvia."

"True."

As we mused over that point of esoteric wisdom, Solly Steinberg was paged for a telephone call.

"That's you," Scotty pointed out.

"No it isn't. If they want me, they can page Murray Roberts. I'll be damned if I'll let these queens get onto my real name."

A couple of minutes later they paged Murray Roberts.

"Hello?"

"I gather we don't answer to Solly in the bars?" said the voice of Jimmy Coleman.

"You gather right. Why are you calling me here?"

"Your aunt just called me and wondered if I might have any idea where you and one of *those* people might be having lunch."

"And you had an idea."

"And I told her," he said, a hint of a giggle warping his baritone.

"You did *what?*"

Now he was positively laughing. "I also told her how to get there. She should be arriving any minute. Just thought I'd warn you. See you at two!"

The phone went dead in my hand.

I ordered more drinks for Scott and myself. While I was debating the pros and cons of warning him of the impending doom, the point went moot.

Aunt Sylvia entered the lion's den.

Fortunately the Gold Rush is very dark and it takes a minute or two before you can see anybody. On more than one occasion I've taken advantage of that moment to hide behind a pillar. It didn't seem worth it this time, though.

"Guess who's coming to lunch?" I whispered.

"If it's that ass you were dating last month, count me out," Scotty mumbled. "Married men from the East Bay who want you to do a Back Street number aren't my scene. Besides, you look like hell in wedgies." (All right, so I'd broken Rule One. But I didn't know it until it was too late.)

"Don't worry," I replied. "Ever since I told him to fuck off he pretends like I'm invisible. I stepped on his toe the other day, and he didn't even react. Aunt Sylvia."

"What about her?" (After a few drinks, Scotty's a little slow on the uptake.)

"That's who's coming to lunch."

"You're shitting me!"

"Be charming," I said. "Here she comes."

Scott was charmingly bolting his drink and waving frantically at Ivan for another fast one when Aunt Sylvia hove to.

"Solly, you don't mind I should join you for lunch?" she said, all wide-eyed like a barracuda. "I just happened to be downtown, and I came in here by accident, and—"

"I just talked to Dr. Coleman," I mentioned.

"—there you were. . . . Why were you talking to him?"

"He called me to tell me you were on your way."

"Conversations with doctors are supposed to be private."

"I'm the patient, not you."

She ignored this and turned to other things. "So aren't you going to introduce me to your friend?"

I made the introductions.

"Murray's told me so much about you," Scott cooed, making with the big smile and the firm hand-shake.

"Your friend doesn't look queer," said Aunt Sylvia by way of an opening compliment. Scott blanched.

"Look, Mary-Louise, tell your aunt—" he began. But I cut him off.

"Why don't we go into the dining room?" I suggested.

"Why don't we?" Scott agreed, somewhat icily.

Scott led the way, looking like he was rehearsing a major address on Gay Rights to deliver with the soup. Aunt Sylvia followed, with me bringing up the rear. Several friends and acquaintances had the good sense not to speak. We got a table fast.

Aunt Sylvia surveyed the room.

"Where are the girls?" she wanted to know.

"All around you," Scott said, scowling into the near-est drink. I don't think it was his, but who cared?

"Oh," said Aunt Sylvia, retreating into the menu.

I tried to figure out what she wanted to be there for.

Scott tried to figure out how soon he could get out of there.

Aunt Sylvia tried to figure out what she wanted to eat.

Conversation during lunch was desultory, to say the least. It was filled with long silences suddenly broken by all three of us speaking at once. A bunch of "you firsts," and "after yous" would follow, and then an-other long silence.

By one thirty Scott and I were both smashed, and Aunt Sylvia was fed.

"Well," she said. "Such a good lunch for a place like this. Don't forget to check the bill."

"Yes, Aunt Sylvia," I said through clenched teeth.

"Watch the pennies . . ."

". . . and the dollars will take care of themselves," I finished for her.

"How delightfully Jewish," Scott said. "Did you learn that on the kibbutz?"

Aunt Sylvia looked blank; Zionism is not her bag. "You better get to the doctor, Solly," she said. "What time will you be home?"

"I don't know," I replied. "Scott and I were sort of planning . . ."

"Oh, I forgot to tell you," Scott jumped in, all malice. "I can't make it tonight. I have a date with the girl I met last night."

Aunt Sylvia lit up.

"You have a girl?"

"Didn't Murray tell you?" Scott purred. "She's charming. West Indian, and working her way through school."

"So? Working? Her family won't help her?"

"Her family's very poor, I'm afraid. She lives down on Sixth Street." (I could have killed him.)

"Is that a nice neighborhood?" Aunt Sylvia asked.

"It depends on what you like," Scotty said smoothly. "Maybe you'd like to meet her. I could bring her over tonight, and perhaps she has a friend who would like to meet Murray."

I lashed out at Scott under the table while Aunt Sylvia was telling him what a wonderful idea it was, and didn't I agree.

Well, what could I say? Naturally, I had to agree. And naturally I had to trust to Scott's good taste and sense not to pursue the matter.

A dumb trust, if ever there was one.

I spent an idle hour with Jimmy Coleman, sparring about what he seemed to think were my neuroses, then took the rest of the afternoon off. By the time I got home, Aunt Sylvia had prepared the kind of dinner that I learned to loathe years ago. Knishes, and borscht, and the ubiquitous brisket, and God knows what else. The only thing that wasn't there was chicken soup, and I happen to like chicken soup.

All during dinner, Aunt Sylvia went on about how charming Scott was (mainly because he had a "girl friend") and how with friends like that there was still hope for me. Along about eight, the doorbell rang.

There they were. Scotty, dead drunk but looking stone sober, and with him was the most beat-up looking Mexican hooker in San Francisco.

She must have been in her twenties, but she looked every day of forty-five. She had the same kind of svelte figure as a young hippopotamus, and her beady little eyes peered myopically through five sets of heavily mascaraed lashes. She'd painted her face within an inch of whatever life was left in it, and it was obvious that Scott hadn't been kidding when he said he'd awakened in a mass of tits that morning. She had enough boob for four Farrah Fawcetts, and none of it was being supported by a bra.

Also, she was as drunk as Scotty.

"Aaaaaaah!" she squealed. "Joo got nize 'pot-ment."

They came in.

"This is Lupe. All her friends were busy tonight," Scott apologized. "I hope you don't mind us coming alone."

"Would it do me any good?"

"Not really. Where's your charming aunt?" The two of them lurched into the hall, and the floor creaked.

"If you mean Aunt Sylvia," I hissed, "she's in the living room. Why don't you two just go on upstairs and sully my sheets?" (Better to have the sheets sullied than for Aunt Sylvia to lay eyes on Lupe.)

"Aunt Sylvia wants to meet my girl, remember?" Scott leered.

"Solly, who is it?" Aunt Sylvia called from the living room.

"It's Scott, but he can't stay," I called back.

"What joo mean, not stay?" Lupe squalled. She whirled on Scott. "Joo promised me three-way!"

I died a little, but not enough to forget what was happening. Aunt Sylvia appeared in the hall.

"Leave? What's this with leave? They just got here. Come in. Sit. Have some Cel-Ray tonic."

She'd grabbed the cow by the foreleg and was dragging her toward the living room. I could see the furniture dissolving under the overload, but managed to squeeze in first and point the mass toward the most substantial piece of furniture in the place. (In case anybody's interested, a Miës van der Rohe Barcelona chair doesn't hold up very well under three hundred pounds of hooker.) I sat mutely while Aunt Sylvia and Scott made polite conversation.

Lupe made occasional guttural sounds and smashed a Waterford ashtray.

Eventually, they left.

I kept my eyes closed as long as I could. I mean, who

needs to see the wrath of a Jewish aunt, a bent Barcelona, and eighty dollars' worth of broken crystal all at once?

"So she's a little overweight, and wears too much makeup," Aunt Sylvia said. "A good diet, and a few lessons on how to . . ."

I left the room without a word. Apparently, as far as Aunt Sylvia is concerned, *any* girl is better than a man.

I want the psychiatrist; Aunt Sylvia will settle for the prostitute.

16

On Friday, Aunt Sylvia went home. All right, so I put in an emergency call to Uncle Hymie to have him call her back to Beverly Hills. What's wrong with that? Isn't that what uncles are for? To protect you from aunts? Call it an extension of the avuncular relationship. Call it anything you want—at least it got rid of Aunt Sylvia.

Naturally she had parting words for me.

"Keep seeing Dr. Coleman."

(I certainly hope so!)

"Try to develop an interest in girls."

(I certainly hope *not!*)

"Try not to be unhappy."

(Who's unhappy? She's leaving, isn't she?)

I assured her that I'd do my best on all counts and hustled her off to the airport. Then I went looking for Scott.

Scott was stone sober, at home, and doing some cleaning. I wasn't sure it was Scott till I saw the whites of his eyes. They were red: it was Scott.

"I suppose you want to talk about last night," he said, obviously not wanting to talk about it himself.

"We don't have to talk about it. Just write me a check for five hundred dollars, and we'll forget it ever happened."

"Five hundred dollars?" he squawked. "What for?"

"The chair and the ashtray. Some of us don't live surrounded by junk. Some of us have nice things." The implication was wasted.

"Do you take Master Charge?" Scott wanted to know.

"No, and your clap card from the health department isn't any good either. I take it you don't have the money?"

"If I had any money I'd get the hell out of town," Scott complained. "Harry wants to throw me out, and the hooker wants to move in."

I sat down and demanded a drink.

"Don't tell me you brought her home last night?" This strained all credulity.

"All right, I won't tell you," Scott sulked, pouring the drinks.

"Jesus," I told him. "That must have been great. You live with the Yellow Rose of Texas, and present him with a hooker who happens to be Mexican."

"It could have been worse," Scott pointed out. "As it happens, I caught him with not one, not two, but three—count them *three*—hustlers in the house."

"Shall I ask what they were doing, or would I prefer not to know?"

"They were all drunk, and Houston Harriet was passed out. If I hadn't gotten here when I did, they'd have stolen everything in the place."

"What do you care," I reminded him. "It's all Harry's anyway."

"That's not the point. Anyway, I threw them out, then Lupe and I finished off the liquor and went to bed. That's where Harriet found us this morning."

"I gather you didn't go to work?" I asked.

"What does it look like I'm doing right now?"

"Not much, if you want the truth."

"I don't. Fix me another drink while I finish dusting."

I mixed; Scott dusted.

Then he threw in the dustcloth, sank to the sofa, and gulped half the drink. "Ooooh," he sighed. "I may survive. Where was I?"

"Harry had just found you and the human half of the donkey act in the sack together."

"Oh. Can't we skip that part?"

"Why? It can't be any tawdrier than the rest of the story."

"Why go into the details?" Scott said. "It all boils down to the fact that I have to find someplace else to live."

"How soon?"

"Oh, there's no rush. Anytime before Harriet gets home from work will be fine."

"In other words, you're planning on moving in with me again, right?"

"Only for a few days."

"With you, a few days always turns out to be several months. Anyway, it seems like several months." Then a thought struck me. "Question: if you're leaving, why are you cleaning the place?"

"I want to make Harry feel bad. Besides, I'm going to leave everything here till I find a place to live."

"That's good," I said. "You I can stand. Your furniture, I can't."

"God, you're piss-elegant," Scotty sneered.

"I spent years learning how." I finished the drink and stood up. "If you're moving in, throw some things in a suitcase and let's go. I don't want to be here when Harry gets home."

"I don't either. Call a cab—I've already packed. All I have to do is throw my toothbrush and razor in my trick-bag."

So there we were, just Fritzie and Mitzie and Scotty and me. Scotty insisted we go out that night to celebrate his divorce (I hadn't even known he and Harry were lovers!), but I really wasn't into it.

About eleven I, for reasons still unknown, decided to make a return appearance at the Rendezvous, where one doesn't normally go after one turns thirty. Granted, I was lying about my age, but on the other hand, after going there fourteen years, they would have known I was lying at one end or the other. Anyway, off I went.

I hiked up the stairs with only one rest stop (another reason not to go there after thirty) and there I stood, stunning Murray Roberts, back after a four-year absence. I paused on the platform in the foyer and surveyed the crowd. All of a sudden there he was—a gorgeous young number, not more than twenty-one or -two, and he was looking directly at me.

Aha! I thought. You're going to make out tonight.

I elbowed my way to the bar, wedged my way in next to the gorgeous young number, and ordered a drink. Then I went into my nonchalant act.

I glanced at the young number.

He glanced at me.

I smiled.

He smiled.

I asked him if he wanted to dance.

He did.

We danced.

We peered into each other's eyes, and he whispered into my ear.

"I think older men are *so* attractive."

All right, I told myself, don't get upset. He's young. Still, he could have said *mature* men. On the other hand, he meant it as a compliment, so I forgave him.

When he went on to tell me that he thought baldness was sexy, I left. My hair may be thinning a little in back, but I am *not* bald.

I took my ego back to Polk Street for a little bolstering, and found Scott more or less where I'd left him.

"You back?" I could tell from his tone he wasn't really interested.

"Guess what?" I asked.

"What?"

"I've just been called an older man."

"I warned you not to go to the Rendezvous. Once we reach twenty-five, we lose our visas for that place. How was it?"

"Not like when we used to go there," I said as nastily as I could. "They all dress like slobs now, and their conversation consists of a series of 'Oh, wows!' and 'Heavys!' Also, they looked dirty. Except for the number who called me an older man."

"How old was *he?*"

"Twenty-one. Twenty-two."

"My dear," Scott told me with an air of authority, "to someone that age, you *are* an older man. Did he want your body?"

"Oh, who cares?" I said. "I didn't want his by the time I'd talked to him a couple of minutes."

"Do I smell sour grapes?"

"Fuck you and the sour grapes, too," I snarled, and stomped out. I grabbed a cab and went to a little bar on Upper Grant, where I sat until two in the morning listening to Edith Piaf and sipping Flor d'Alp. Up there, people leave you alone. If they don't, the woman who owns the place chases them out with a tennis racket.

When I got home, I thought I'd have a drink with Scotty and apologize for telling him to fuck himself, but there were two heads on his pillow, so I didn't disturb him. Besides, from what I saw of the other head, Scott must really have been drunk that night. Either that, or Scott likes *much* older men.

I decided to take Mitzie and Fritzie out for a walk, then go home to bed. It was two thirty, and I was worn out from a long day.

Or was I just worn out?

17

Well, I survived the week, and I have to say, it made me appreciate Uncle Hymie all the more. I mean, the man must be a saint if he lives with Aunt Sylvia all the time. (Maybe he hires a bunch of aging Jewish character actors, and they all take turns being Uncle Hymie.) Anyway, the week proved one thing—am I ever glad I'm not straight. If I were straight, I'd have to marry a nice Jewish girl (no excuses accepted) and if they all turn out like Aunt Sylvia——? I wonder if she was always like she is, or if it's something that comes with menopause? What am I saying? If it was something that came with menopause, she wouldn't have been like she was when I was a kid, but she was.

I didn't know what Aunt Sylvia might tell Uncle Hymie about his case, so I wrote him a note telling him the whole thing was dropped, and if he gets a bill he should pay it.

Actually, I came through the week relatively unscarred, although I lost a couple of clients. Not that it mattered—San Francisco is full of women with more money than brains, and any young man with a little taste and a resale license can clean up. Come to think of it, taste isn't really all that necessary. All you have to be is heavy into flocked wallpaper and art nouveau, and you've got it made, although I have a feeling plastic kelp may be *de rigueur* next year.

Saturday night I went out to dinner with Jimmy Coleman, and then dancing after dinner. It was all very strange—for some reason, the usual Murray Roberts bright conversation disappeared, and was replaced by good old Solly Steinberg, and his klutzy chatter. Also, and don't ask me why, I had an attack of diarrhea, which kept me hopping. By the time the evening came to an end, I wasn't about to ask him to come home with me (God only knew what might happen, my bowels being what they were) and he didn't ask me to his house, either. I decided maybe he didn't like me, though he did make another date for the next weekend.

Sunday I spent recovering from Saturday night, and Monday I got a letter from Aunt Sylvia:

Dear Solly, [Things must not be too bad!]

Hymie tells me I should write and thank you for having me in your home, but I say why should I thank you? Isn't it a nephew's duty to give shelter to his Aunt who raised him anymore? So to keep peace in the family, I thank you for your hospitality. I wish I could tell you I liked your apartment, but the truth is, it didn't seem to me like the sort of place a man would feel comfortable in.

Where, for instance, is your broken-down easy

chair that should have been thrown out years ago?

And why aren't there piles of dirt in the corners? Did you clean it especially for me? You didn't have to do that—I would have been happy to clean your house even though I was only a couple of days out of the hospital and needed the complete rest I wish I could have gotten.

And why do you live on a hill? Are there maybe no nice places that aren't going to slide into the Bay with the first good earthquake? Do you walk up that hill twice a day like I did? You'll get yourself a heart attack, God willing you don't get mugged when you stay out so late every night.

What's so interesting about the middle of the night that you can't get a good night's sleep now and then? The weekends are maybe not enough for you?

I'd say what you need is to get married, but I'm afraid that's a dream I'm going to have to learn to live without. I only pray that someday you can be happy.

I've been thinking about your friend Scott. (Don't tell me anymore that I don't care about your queer friends—I thought Scott was very nice, but I really can't understand what I said at the restaurant that upset him.) Anyway, I think you should cultivate Scott and that nice girl of his. Granted, she could stand to lose a few pounds, and it would be nice if she'd shave her legs and armpits, but she seemed to be a good-hearted girl. All right, so she's a little clumsy—nobody's perfect. Anyway, I can't help but think that maybe if you got to know her you might learn to appreciate the virtues of the fairer sex. Not that I'm trying to run your life. Dr. Coleman says I shouldn't do that, and I won't. But a little well-meant advice never hurt, right? Of course, right!

Try to get more sleep, and take better care of yourself. Who knows? Maybe your problem is just that you're tired.

Love,
Aunt Sylvia

Tired! Boy, was I tired! Tired of taking Aunt Sylvia's well-meant advice is what I was tired of. (That she might be a little tired of taking mine never occurred to me, but that's getting ahead of things.) Anyway, I sat down and wrote her a long letter, which I decided was going to be my last. If she didn't get the message this time, she wasn't going to get it at all. What I told her, basically, was this:

So you thought that girl of Scotty's was nice? Aunt Sylvia, what that girl was, was a broken-down hooker from south of Market. And as for what it was that offended Scott, you said he didn't "look like a queer." This is a compliment? Aunt Sylvia, this is not a compliment—this is an insult! Apparently you didn't notice, but we don't all look alike. We look just like everyone else, which is probably why most straights think there are a lot less of us than there are. The invisible minority, that's what they call us. So, if we're invisible, how do they know we're a minority? The way the closets are emptying these days, it might turn out

[136]

that the straights are the minority! How would you like that, Aunt Sylvia? Can't you just see it? There you and Uncle Hymie are, minding your own business, having a sandwich at the deli, when all of a sudden the cops appear, load you into the paddy wagon, and Uncle Hymie is hoping his boss won't find out he's straight. . . .

I have also gotten the distinct impression that you have been getting your information about us gay types from those books with "colonated" titles—things like *Homosexuality: Sick or Sinful?*— usually written by a couple of doctors (traveling in pairs on the theory that there's safety in numbers), and filled with all the gory emergency-room stories, and case histories of suicidal gay people.

The idea usually seems to be that the only thing that is keeping us all alive is our ongoing search for the perfect penis, which, if we don't find it by a week from next Wednesday, we're going to kill ourselves over. And the search, of course, is always being conducted in parks and men's rooms. Aunt Sylvia, if this were true, do you realize that there would be lines of men outside every public toilet in the country, and the parks would be so jammed there wouldn't be any room for the bushes we are all supposed to be making it under?

All right, so there *are* men who cruise tearooms and parks. But does your average straight child molester operate solely in the confines of the bedroom? Maybe he puts a sign on the front lawn— "The Pervert Is In: Five-Year-Olds Welcome."

There also seems to be a feeling that most of us spend what little time we have left after our park and pissoir sessions making it with cucumbers.

I gather that an occasional doctor must have yanked a cucumber or a carrot out of a queen. Well, before we all get written off as freaks, someone better check the records on what hospitals have been known to remove from the insides of women. Everything from bobby pins to gin bottles. Aunt Sylvia, are you willing to take the rap because some woman in the next town stuffed a neon tube up herself? Tell you what, Aunt Sylvia —I'll refrain from thinking such things of you, and you do the same for me.

Then there's all the nonsense about the transience of gay relationships, which usually involves a couple of theories, used interchangeably: (1) Gay relationships don't last because we're all so sick to start with; and (2) because the relationships don't last, we all become terminally neurotic. A no-win proposition if there ever was one.

So how are the relationships going to last? Do we have our families nagging us to work it out? To stay together for the children's sake? To think of the alimony if we split up? Do we get loaded down with a mass of wedding presents that it's easier to live with together than to divide up? Hah! What we get are a bunch of Aunt Sylvias smiling weakly and telling their friends that we "aren't the marrying kind."

Now I ask you, Aunt Sylvia. How many marriages do you think would work out if they had to be hidden from the families, hidden from the world, and generally sneered at by eighty percent of the population?

How many marriages work out, even with plenty of support?

Take a look at the divorce rate, then think what it would be if the only thing involved in a divorce were for one or the other to simply pack up and move out?

How many men do you know who stay with their wives only because they can't afford to support two households?

How many women do you know who stay with their husbands only because they are incapable of supporting themselves?

How many couples do you know who stay together only because of the children?

You want the truth about gay people, Aunt Sylvia? Think of everything you know about straight people, and straight relationships, sexual and otherwise. Now substitute another man for the woman involved, or another woman for the man involved. And you know what happens? Nothing, Aunt Sylvia. The same problems, the same pleasures, with one exception.

We can't reproduce.

So with the overpopulation in the world, that in itself should make people pro-gay.

Well, I think I've said all I have to say on that subject, Aunt Sylvia.

Jimmy Coleman tells me he thinks I've been a little rough on you, and I guess he's right. (It seems like no matter what the subject, Jimmy is usually right, which can sometimes be annoying!) I guess I've told you some things maybe you didn't want to know. On the other hand, I notice you're not in the hospital, so things can't be too bad.

Maybe I've been trying to punish you for some

reason, or make you feel as bad as you've sometimes made me feel. But you weren't trying to
make me feel bad. You were only trying to do
what you thought was right. I suppose it isn't your
fault if you hurt me—you didn't know what you
were doing. On the other hand, now you know. So
please, Aunt Sylvia, no more hints that I would be
better off straight, no more assumptions that I'm
miserable. I'm not miserable, not any more than
anybody else, and I wouldn't want to be straight.
And please, don't ask me if I'd want my own son
to be gay.

Barring unforeseen accidents, I'm not going to
have a son.

So I'm serving notice, Aunt Sylvia.

No more slurs.

No more breast-beating.

No more shit.

Talk it over with Uncle Hymie. Talk it over with
your doctor. Talk it over with yourself. Then decide whether you still want to be my loving aunt.
If you don't, then please drop me a postcard. I
have enough problems coping with the stupidities
of intolerant straights every day of my life. I don't
have to put up with it from my family, too.

I'd rather find a new family.

I signed the letter with love, and sent it off, figuring
that I would either hear an explosion from the south,
or nothing at all. What was really happening, I didn't
find out about until a lot later, and if I'd known it was
going on when it was going on, I'd probably have been
angry as hell.

18

Aunt Sylvia, apparently, decided she couldn't talk my letter over with Uncle Hymie, or her doctor, or herself. No, she decided she could only talk it over with *my* doctor, so she sent it along to Jimmy Coleman, who, naturally, didn't bother to tell me he'd seen it, or was commenting on it to Aunt Sylvia.

What he did was this. He read the letter, told Aunt Sylvia that he basically agreed with what I'd said (bless his gorgeous blue eyes!), and suggested to her, in terms that would have been clear to anybody but Aunt Sylvia, that she really should discuss things with Marvin Pomerantz. Then he went on to tell her that maybe things would be easier for her if she stopped thinking of me as Solly Steinberg, and started thinking of me as Murray Roberts. His theory, which I had never thought of, was that Solly Steinberg was the little boy Aunt Sylvia thought she was raising, while Murray Roberts was the man that little boy turned out to be. He pointed out to her that while she had all kinds of preconceived notions about Solly, she didn't know anything at all about Murray, but if she gave him a chance, she might like him.

Then he told her again to go talk to Marvin Pomerantz, and left things to her.

Well, it must have been a scene. When I finally heard about it, I could see it perfectly:

There's Mrs. Pomerantz's son-the-doctor, sitting innocently behind his desk, when in comes Aunt Sylvia. She sits down, and starts fidgeting. Mrs. Pomerantz's son-the-doctor begins asking questions, trying to determine just which of Aunt Sylvia's imaginary illnesses is acting up this time, when Aunt Sylvia, in her usual tactful way, says:

"Marvin Pomerantz, are you queer?"

He cringes, remembers that his lover chops her hair once a week, and wonders why she's asking such a question at this late date. So he nods his head.

"Does your mother know about this?" Aunt Sylvia asks.

Again, Mrs. Pomerantz's son-the-doctor nods his head, not having a ready answer for such a question, this being a subject they didn't cover in medical school.

"What does she think about it?" Aunt Sylvia goes on. Finally young Marvin finds his voice.

"Think about it?" he says, somewhat inanely. "I'm not sure what you mean."

"Marvin Pomerantz," Aunt Sylvia thunders. "I asked you a simple question in plain English. They maybe didn't teach you English in college? I should write the question in Latin on a prescription pad, maybe? What does your mother think about your being gay?"

"Look, Mrs. Leiberman," Marvin stammers, "maybe you'd better tell me what this is all about."

So she did. Oh, boy, did she tell him. The whole schmeer. Not, of course, that it came as any great surprise to him, he having talked to Uncle Hymie, and having recommended Jimmy Coleman in the first place.

What it boiled down to was that Aunt Sylvia wanted to talk things over with someone her own age and her own sex, and she thought maybe Rachel Pomerantz would be a good one to talk things over with.

Marvin hears her out, then looks her straight in the eye (which, you have to admit, takes guts).

"Mrs. Leiberman," he says. "I'm sure Mother wouldn't mind having a chat with you, but if you think she's going to join you in one of those sessions of 'what-am-I-going-to-do,' you'd better be prepared. She's much more likely to start bragging about Bill and me, and show you our income tax returns for last year."

Aunt Sylvia, holding true to form, gives Marvin one of her best glares, and stomps out. Marvin Pomerantz picks up the phone, calls Jimmy Coleman, and invites himself and his lover to San Francisco for the weekend, which he says is going to be Jimmy's penance for telling Aunt Sylvia he's gay. Also he threatens to bring the whole thing up before the AMA as a subject for debate: "Question to the Convention: Is It Ethical to Squeal on Your Ex-Lover to One of His Patients?"

Also, he asks Jimmy if I am still "the nelly little kid with glasses" he knew so many years ago. I never did like Marvin Pomerantz!

Well, time marched on, as it usually does, and then one day I found a letter from Aunt Sylvia in my mailbox. I took the letter in, stared at it for a long time, and fixed myself a drink.

The letter was a long one.

Dear Murray, [What is this? I fixed another drink.]

So don't go get a new family, already. Notice I did not start this letter Dear Solly. [I noticed! I noticed!] I guess the Solly I knew, or at least hoped I knew, was just a figment of my imagination. So good-bye, Solly. Hello, Murray.

Only it isn't that easy. I probably just won't call you anything for a while. Besides, who ever heard of a Jewish aunt with a nephew named Murray Roberts? Morris, maybe, but Murray? So, I'll try to get used to it.

I can't really say I understand what's going on —I wish I could. It seems like all of a sudden I find out that all my life I've been surrounded with gay people. Please notice that I did not say "queer."

So how was I to know? It's not like you wear signs—maybe it would be better if you did. At least that way people would know that you're just like everybody else, not like Paul Lynde and Truman Capote. Are they gay? They sure act like it.

Except anymore I'm not so sure what *it's* like.

I mean, I certainly never would have expected Dr. Coleman to turn out to be gay, which he didn't tell me, but I eventually figured out for myself, like I eventually figured it out about Marvin Pomerantz. Solly—I mean Murray—do you know I've been going to a gay doctor for almost five years now?

All right, so I haven't died, so he must be a good doctor.

Let me tell you, when I walked into his office and sat right down and faced him with it, I thought he was going to die. Such a red face you've never seen. So then I had to tell him all about why I wanted to know (naturally I had to tell him about you, I hope you don't mind) and I asked him what his mother thought about him being gay, and if he thought maybe I could talk to her about it. So he told me I should.

That's not so easy as it sounds. Like what was I supposed to do, call her up and say, "So, Rachel, how's by your son the homosexual?"

You'll be happy to know that's not what I did. Instead I called her up and told her I had a problem I wanted to discuss with her.

"With me?" she said, like I was some kind of stranger. "For ten years we've known each other, and now you want to discuss a problem with me? Why don't you call Miriam Levitz? I thought she was supposed to be your best friend." To talk to Miriam Levitz, I don't think is the best idea, but I didn't tell Rachel why.

"This problem, Rachel," I said, "I can discuss only with you. So will you come over and have some coffee and Danish?"

"If I have to discuss a problem, I like to be at home. You come over here."

So I went over there. What is with Rachel? It was my problem. Why shouldn't we discuss it in my home? Well, Rachel was always like that.

"So what is it?" she said when I'd sat down. "Is it something with Hymie?"

[145]

I shook my head.

"Is it something with Solly?"

I nodded.

"Maybe we're going to play twenty questions?"

I shook my head again. I mean, what could I say?

"Sylvia," she said. "Look at me." I looked. "Now, tell me, Sylvia, what is the problem? It can't be so bad you can't talk about it. With people like us, *nothing* is so bad we can't talk about it."

"Solly's a homosexual," I blurted out.

"So?" Rachel said. "Is that the big problem? Who's it a big problem for? You, or Solly?"

"What do you mean?"

"Just what I said. Who's having the problem? You, or Solly?"

I hadn't really thought about it, but I guessed it was me that was having the problem. "I am, I guess," I said.

"Hah!" said Rachel. "That's what I thought. So what's your big problem all about? You think you got problems? You got a good husband with a good job, you got a good home, and you got a good nephew. So what are your problems? You afraid maybe you should be ashamed of Solly?"

"Why not?" I said. "I never raised him to be . . ."

"So who's to say how you raised him? Sylvia, you're only responsible for getting him grown. You're not responsible for how he lives his life. So what skin is it off your teeth who he sleeps with? You'd rather maybe he was picking up prostitutes?"

"Rachel, are you saying you approve of these homosexuals?"

"Who's to approve or disapprove? What can I do about it? I should maybe disinherit my own son? Look, Sylvia, I only had one son. So now I got two. Who needs a daughter-in-law anyway? All you can do with them is tell them what lousy housekeepers they are. You should see the place Marvin and Bill have. Spotless!

"I'm telling you, you could eat off their floor if it weren't that the china is nicer. And does Bill resent me? Ha! Now there's a boy that appreciates a Jewish mother. Marvin I always think wishes I would maybe butt out now and then. So I go to Bill, and he takes care of Marvin for me. Now I ask you, how many other people do you know that can say that? Hunh, Sylvia?"

"But I always wanted grandchildren . . ."

"Grandchildren! What's with grandchildren? You take Miriam Levitz. What does she have from her grandchildren? Wet diapers, and gifts twice a year that she has to throw away because they leak. Also, babysitting, which is no joy when you consider the number of weekends Sam is in San Francisco doing God-knows-what!" (I knew, but wasn't about to tell Rachel!) "All right, so maybe it would be fun to have a baby around the house for an evening now and then. But what happens? You get stuck with them for a week at a time while the kids go to Honolulu. Me? I go to Honolulu with Marvin and Bill. So what do I need grandchildren for? Besides which, I should point out that Solly's children would not be your grandchildren, anyway. They'd be grandnieces or grandnephews, or something."

"But what do I tell people?" I wanted to know.

"Tell people? Aha! So that's it. How do you explain why Solly is thirty-four and not married? Why explain? Whose business is it but Solly's? If people get pushy, just tell them as rudely as you can that he's queer. You've told the truth, and nobody will believe you. Anyway, the ones who would get upset wouldn't believe you. They think all gay boys wear fluffy sweaters and tight pants, and they know Solly, and how could anybody that they know be queer? The ones who will believe you, won't care. You'll see. So don't tell me you got problems. You think you got problems, think of the problems Solly's got."

"Solly? Solly claims the only problem he has is me."

"So, Sylvia, maybe he's right?" Rachel says.

So, anyway, you can see how it went.

So, maybe she's right.

Anyway, please try to see your way clear to giving me another chance. I promise I won't try to change you anymore. I guess after thirty-four years, you should be able to make up your own mind what you are and who you are. But after sixty-three years, it's going to take me a little while to adjust. So don't go running out to find a new family quite yet, okay? Of course, okay!

Love,
Aunt Sylvia

19

Let me tell you, that letter was the only bright spot in what had not been an easy day.

To start things off, Scotty had picked up a hustler the night before, and that morning his credit cards were gone, which, frankly, didn't bother me too much. I mean, that was the fourth time it'd happened to him, and if you ask me, I think he should either get rid of them or lock them up. When I suggested it that morning, though, he was too busy sending thirty-four telegrams to his creditors to listen. Thirty-four! What can anyone do with thirty-four credit cards? Get thirty-four times further in debt, that's what.

What bothered me is that it'd been like that since the day he moved in. Such a parade of people had been through my house, even I didn't believe. So far, I'd lost two candlesticks (fake), some silverware (plate), and a cigarette lighter (broken). Nothing terribly serious, but if things escalated, I was going to have to take steps. It's not that I minded him bringing people home; I just wished he'd start bringing home a better class of people. Oh, well, I guess he just wanted what he wanted, and who was I to tell him he was wrong. Besides, when he saw them in the morning, he usually realized he'd made a mistake. The problem was that instead of escorting them to the door, he just buried his head in the pillow, and hoped they'd go away. Which they did, taking everything with them that wasn't nailed down. At any rate, that morning one of my better lithographs was missing, and I had decided it was time to take him in hand, introduce him to a better class of people, and hope one of *them* would take *him* home for a change.

After I got done chastising Scotty, Mrs. Jordan called and starting complaining that her bedroom curtains weren't hanging right. Well, what did she expect, demanding that I make curtains out of aluminum foil? She thought maybe they'd hang like Prussian pouffes? So I went over there and uncrumpled them as best I could, and charged her thirty dollars an hour for my time. (She complained, but I pointed out there are no fixed rates for foil flatteners. She'll only get tired of them soon—they may cast interesting reflections, but when the wind blows they sound like rattlesnakes.)

So, as I said, Aunt Sylvia's letter was the only bright spot, and I had to agree with her that it would take a while for her to adjust to things. What the hell—I'd been adjusting for thirty-four years, so I figured she was entitled to a week or two.

What was really worrying me was Jimmy Coleman. Something very weird was going on there. Every time I was with him, I'd have a good time, but for some reason I never seemed to be able to come out with the old "you-want-to-go-home-and-fuck?" line. I mean, what would I have done if he'd said no? If you pull that line in a bar with a stranger and you get turned down, you can always make up all kinds of stories to protect your ego. Maybe the guy has a lover at home. Or maybe he's tired. Or maybe he has the clap. Anything but "maybe I don't turn him on."

But if I propositioned Jimmy Coleman, and he turned me down, it was going to hurt. Worse, I began to worry that he might not turn me down, but I might bomb out in the sack. Not that I'd ever had that problem, but it could happen. I mean, I've heard of such things happening, and it did not sound so great. What would I do? And what would he do? If there was one guy I didn't want leaving in the middle of the night, it was Jimmy Coleman.

Also, I was beginning to wonder about what it would be like to fix orange juice for him in the morning. It occurred to me that it would probably be very nice, until I began to see the rest of the picture.

Like Scott dragging some moron out about eleven, and start to pour gin into himself. That's the trouble with having a roommate: even if they don't embarrass you, their tricks do.

I decided to do a Scarlett O'Hara number, and worry about Jimmy the next day. I had a date with him that night (should I wear Missy Ellen's best portieres?) and I could hardly wait to tell him about Aunt Sylvia's letter. Also, I was hoping I could think up a sneaky way to find out how he was feeling about me, without having to risk telling him how I was feeling about him.

It was beginning to look like maybe I was falling in love.

I couldn't figure out what was going on with Jimmy, so I kept my cards close to my chest.

I kept busy with work, and it seemed like everybody had decided to redecorate—including Jimmy.

One night over dinner he suddenly announced that he wanted his apartment redone, and wondered if I would do it.

Would I? You bet I would. Particularly when he told me I could do it any way I wanted.

Naturally I didn't charge him for the job. For one thing, it was worth it not to have to do something awful just because someone had bad taste. Jimmy didn't seem to have any taste, good or bad. His whole place was filled with all kinds of things he'd picked up here and there in his life, and a lot of what I did was just drag Jimmy out of his trunks and hang him on the wall. I also got him some new furniture (he had that easy chair Aunt Sylvia thought I should have; I threw it out), but mostly it was just a matter of rearranging things. When I got through, though, everybody would know exactly who lived there, which is the way a home should be. A reflection of the occupants. Unfortunately, too many people think a home should be a stage set on which to play out the tawdry little dramas of their lives. Not Jimmy, though. His life isn't a tawdry little drama, and his home didn't turn out to be a stage set. In fact, the way it turned out, I like his place better than my own.

Then one night I ran into Sam Levitz. Jimmy and I were down on Folsom Street (he was doing a monograph on the leather set for some convention) and there was Sam in the Raunch Room. He promptly asked me about Aunt Sylvia and Uncle Hymie, and asked me to say hello to them. It seems he didn't think he'd be seeing much of them anymore, since he'd met someone in San Francisco and finally decided to chuck the whole thing with Miriam and the family and move up here. We met his friend, who looks just like Sam. Between the two of them they were draped in enough leather and chains to clothe a whole chapter of the Hell's Angels. He seemed happy, though, and I figured that counted for something, so the next day I dropped Aunt Sylvia and Uncle Hymie a note, filling them in on why they weren't seeing much of Sam anymore. To test the waters, I described Jimmy's apartment. Then, just to frost the cake, I mentioned that if Aunt Sylvia was planning to either get sick or have her hair done in the near future, she should do it right away, since Marvin and Bill were planning a trip to San Francisco next month.

Since I had heard nothing from Beverly Hills since the last letter, I figured this note might get me a hint as to what was going on. It did.

Dear Murray, [Okay, so far!]

I was wondering about Sam Levitz. Miriam was over here last week, and said she thought she was losing Sam. Losing him? Ha! She lost him years ago, she should never know it. So I asked her what she thought was wrong, and she said maybe he had a girl friend in San Francisco, since he stayed a couple of days longer than he usually does.

"San Francisco?" I said. "In San Francisco it's boyfriends they have."

"What?" Miriam asked. "Are you saying my Sam is maybe a queer?"

"Well, who's to know?"

"I'm to know," she said. "He's my husband.

You think maybe I wouldn't know if he was fooling around with boys?"

"How would you know?"

"A woman always knows," she said. So now I see what Rachel meant when she said people who would get upset don't generally figure things out very fast. Anyway, I dropped the whole thing. If Miriam can figure it all out for herself, fine. But if she can't, why should I stir things up? So she could make life miserable for Sam? I got nothing against Sam Levitz, not after what he did for Hymie. Besides, shouldn't Sam be allowed to live his life any way he wants? What Miriam doesn't know won't hurt her (or Sam either).

I already know about Marv and Bill going up there for a visit. They were over here for dinner and a game of bridge the other night, and made me promise not to get sick for at least a month. (What do I have to be sick about, I ask you?) Also, Bill said he'd do my hair for free if I beat him at bridge, so naturally I got two slams with Marv as my partner. Not only is he a good doctor, but he knows how to bid his cards. His mother should be proud of him.

In case maybe you had forgotten, next month is Mother's Day. A card I would appreciate, but why don't you come down here and take me out to dinner? Marv and Bill are taking Rachel out, and they thought we could go along with them. (Also, I think they have a friend they want you to meet.) So can you come down? Don't tell me you can't afford it—I know how much money you decorators make.

Hymie just read this letter and said I shouldn't have reminded you about Mother's Day. But what's an aunt for if she can't remind you of things like that that you would probably forget if she didn't remind you? You've forgotten Mother's Day every year so far, so why should I think this year should be any different?

Hymie sends love, and wants to know—if we come up to visit, can we stay with you? He doesn't think he wants to stay at a hotel in San Francisco again, since last time he didn't think he got his money's worth.

Love,
Aunt Sylvia

Needless to say, I had no idea what would happen if I invited Aunt Sylvia and Uncle Hymie, but I decided I might as well give it a whirl. So I told Scott he'd have to vacate the premises for the weekend, which was all right with him, since he'd met someone he was planning to run off to the Russian River with, anyway. Of course, I figured that with my luck he and his friend wouldn't be speaking by the time the weekend rolled around, but in that case I could always pack him off to the baths.

Then I told Jimmy, and he decided he'd like to take us all out to dinner. And when I told him about the invitation for Mother's Day, well, let me tell you, things brightened right up, especially when I told him that his ex wanted to line me up with someone. He got this frozen look on his face, then said that if I was going to L.A. for the weekend, he was going with me. I could have kissed him, but I didn't.

Here I was, seeing a psychiatrist, and instead of getting better, my insecurities were getting worse.

So I had another weekend with my family, and began to wonder what the hell was happening. For years I had been carefully avoiding my family, and now here I was, with three weekends in the last couple of months, and another one coming up the next month. I must say, though, that things were improving.

Their arrival was as usual, with me picking them up at the airport. Scott was still home when we got back, and had drinks ready (leave it to Scotty to have drinks ready). There were many effusive greetings, during which Aunt Sylvia neither mentioned that he doesn't look queer, nor asked about his girl friend. Then his date arrived. At least his taste was improving—the guy was presentable and a few years older than Scott, but then, Scott always did have a sort of a thing for older men. (Let's face it, Scotty was a dirty old man's dream!) Scott wouldn't say where he met George, so I assumed he met him at the baths and didn't press the issue. What the hell—Scott had been going to one of the better tubs lately, so George was probably healthy.

We all made polite conversation for a while, then George and Scott took off in the general direction of Guerneville.

I fixed dinner for the three of us, and managed to impress the hell out of Aunt Sylvia.

"You cooked this yourself?" she said.

"It didn't take a minute," I said, which was the truth. It hadn't taken a minute—it had taken the whole day, but I was damned if I was going to tell her that. She'd have told me I shouldn't have bothered. On the other hand, if I hadn't bothered, she'd have said something like, "What, you can't cook for your own family?" You can't win.

"Not bad," she said, which was tantamount to saying she'd never had a better meal in her life. "You really cooked it yourself?"

"When one doesn't have a wife, one has to fend for one's self. I also made all the curtains in this place."

"You'll make somebody a good wife someday," Uncle Hymie observed. Aunt Sylvia choked on a grape leaf.

"Not at the rate things are going," I said. "The only person I ever see anymore is Jimmy Coleman, and I don't know what's happening with him."

"I didn't think you guys ever had any problems getting each other in bed," Uncle Hymie said. "I thought your problem was getting them out again afterwards."

"Hymie!" (That was Aunt Sylvia, trying to sound shocked, but after those letters I wrote her, it didn't sound very convincing.)

"Sylvia, if the boy were having a problem with a girl friend, we'd try to help him, wouldn't we?"

"This kind of problem he wouldn't be having with

a girl friend. He wouldn't be trying to get her into bed unless he'd married her."

"I wouldn't?" I said. (How would *I* know about such things?)

"All right," Uncle Hymie said. "So we'll talk about it after your aunt's gone to bed."

"No," Aunt Sylvia said, putting her fork down. "We'll talk about it now. I got to get it through my head that Solly—excuse me, Murray—has different kinds of problems than if he were straight. If he were straight, I would try to help him. So he's gay. I've still got to try to help him." She turned to me. "So, it's normal for two guys who are going together to sleep together?"

"It's normal," I said. "Generally, we're sleeping together *before* we're going together!"

"So why aren't you sleeping with him?"

"Because I'm not sure he wants to sleep with me."

Aunt Sylvia's eyes narrowed. "You couldn't maybe ask him?"

"It's not that easy." I squirmed.

"Why not?" Uncle Hymie asked. "I mean, it isn't like you've never asked a man to go to bed with you before."

"With him, it's different. What do I do if he says no?"

"No one's ever said no before?"

"No one I ever cared about."

"I see," said Uncle Hymie, not looking like he saw at all.

"I'm glad you do," said Aunt Sylvia. "Because I don't. But don't worry—we'll figure something out. So when is he coming over? Uncle Hymie hasn't met him yet."

"Not till tomorrow," I said. "He had to go to a meeting tonight."

"So fine," said Aunt Sylvia. "Tonight, we'll be just the three of us, just like when you were growing up."

And she was right—it *was* just like when I was growing up. We spent the whole evening playing Monopoly, and as usual Aunt Sylvia won. She goes at Monopoly like she goes at life: grab everything in sight, build like crazy, and if you go bust, at least you went out in a blaze of glory. The only thing different about that night was that instead of getting blasted on Mogen David, we got stinko on Paul Masson. It was sort of like the difference between Warsaw and Beverly Hills: the decor is different, but the mystique is the same.

Saturday we spent sight-seeing. We did all the smarter shops, hit all the restored neighborhoods, and didn't get home till five thirty. Aunt Sylvia's comment was concise:

"This town wouldn't be much if all the gay people moved out, would it?"

True, very true.

Jimmy arrived for drinks, then announced that he'd made reservations for us at P.S. for dinner.

"Is that all right?" he asked Aunt Sylvia.

"How do I know? Is the food good?"

"Very good." He took a deep breath and sprung the rest of the story. "But it's a gay restaurant."

"So?" said Aunt Sylvia. "It's your money. I should tell you you have to spend it in a straight place?"

Off we went to P.S., and Aunt Sylvia did her best not to rubberneck. She wasn't entirely successful, but who could blame her? The entire royal court of San Francisco was there, in full drag, and slightly tipsy.

"That's Renee," Uncle Hymie said, pointing with a fork. Somehow, he managed to sound very casual.

"She looks like Scott's girl friend," Aunt Sylvia observed. "Does she always wear her tiara upside down?"

"Not so loud," Jimmy cautioned her. "She'll hit you with a barstool. She's a lot butcher than she looks."

"Who's she supposed to be?" Aunt Sylvia asked in her best I-could-care-less-but-I'm-asking-to-be-polite voice.

"She's the Empress de San Francisco."

"Empress?" Aunt Sylvia echoed. "That's an empress? If she's an empress, she should get a new dress. That one has a tear in the armpit."

"He only wears it on special occasions," I said. "Like every weekend."

"He?" Aunt Sylvia squawked. "That's a *he?*"

"Of course," I told her. "The Empress de San Francisco is a drag-queen. Every girl at that table is a boy."

Aunt Sylvia gaped.

"Well, now I've seen it all," she said. "Don't tell me the boys are actually girls. That I couldn't stand!"

"Don't worry," Jimmy reassured her. "Dykes in drag never look that good. They either look like nelly men, or wrestlers."

"There's a difference?" (I couldn't resist.)

Aunt Sylvia ignored me. The Empress had set Aunt Sylvia back a pace or two, but I could tell that as far as she was concerned, if Jimmy Coleman said it, it must be true. She shrugged.

"So seeing is believing. Now I've seen. So let him prance around in a dress with a tear in the armpit like no one should be caught dead in. Me? I'm a very open person. Everybody knows that."

Right, Aunt Sylvia. Of course, right.

Jimmy and I took Aunt Sylvia and Uncle Hymie home, got them safely in, and went out for a drink.

"Well?" I said, when we were safely tucked onto a couple of stools at the C.Q.

"Well, what?" Jimmy replied. (Big help.)

"Do you think she's going to make it?"

Jimmy stared at me like I had the brain of a retarded quail. "Murray, she's made it. Once she catches onto everything, you're going to have a very campy aunt."

"That's all I need. With all the campy sisters I've got, what do I need a campy aunt for?"

"Would you rather have her trying to marry you off to a nice Jewish girl?" (As usual, Jimmy is the voice of reason.)

"God, no," I said. "I got that for years. Better she should camp. But now she'll probably start trying to line me up with nice Jewish boys."

"You'd object?"

I shrugged. "I haven't met a Jewish boy yet worth marrying. What I want never seems to want me."

"What does that mean?"

I almost told him. But then, as usual, I decided not to.

"When I decide to tell you what that means, I'll come to your office and pay you for your time," I said, a bit sulkily.

Jimmy looked kind of crestfallen, but I figured better crestfallen than repulsed. So we finished our drinks and went home. He dropped me off at my place (big thrill!) and when I went in, there was Uncle Hymie, reading a book. He looked up at me.

"What, you're home?"

I fixed myself a nightcap, and slumped into a chair.

"Where else would I be?"

"I thought maybe Jimmy Coleman's?" he said hopefully.

"I should be so lucky."

"Nah," said Uncle Hymie. "Don't worry about it. He's a smart man. He'll figure things out without you pushing him."

"Maybe he already has, and just isn't interested," I suggested.

Uncle Hymie eyed me. "Murray, if he weren't interested in you, would he have taken a whole Saturday night to take your family out? I mean, I don't know how you guys operate, but where I come from, a guy only takes a girl's family out if he's interested in her. I mean, if he's going to get involved with the girl, he wants to look the family over first. Did he like us?"

"He liked you."

"Good. We liked him, too. Let me give you some advice, young man. Nothing makes a Jewish mother happier than for her daughter to marry a doctor or for her son to be one. So why shouldn't a Jewish aunt be happy to see her nephew who obviously isn't going to *be* a doctor, marry one?"

"Don't forget, he's not Jewish," I pointed out.

"Don't forget, he's not a girl," Hymie shot back. "I guess the standards change when it turns out you have nothing against Jewish girls, but it's *any* girls you want nothing to do with."

"Well, the whole subject is academic," I grumbled. "At the rate things are going, nothing is ever going to happen."

"You think so? You seem to forget you got an Aunt Sylvia."

With that he went to bed, and so did I.

21

Sunday morning was looking fairly good—Aunt Sylvia and Uncle Hymie were leaving, and I was beginning to feel safe—when things suddenly turned sour.

Scotty came home, about eight hours early. Actually, if he'd just held off another thirty minutes, everything would have been fine. As it was, we were just finishing breakfast, and I hadn't yet gotten Aunt Sylvia and Uncle Hymie out of the house.

Scotty was not in what you could call prime condition. In fact, he looked like hell. Unshaven, eyes bloodshot, and a certain tremulousness about him that looked terminal until he laced a glass of orange juice with about three parts of vodka, drained it, and sank into a chair.

"You always do that so early in the morning?" Aunt Sylvia asked. Scotty peered at her, somewhat fuzzily.

"It isn't morning yet," he announced. "It's still last night."

"Maybe we should go to the airport," I suggested. I should have saved my breath. Aunt Sylvia dismissed me and my suggestion with one of those gestures that tells you that as far as she is concerned, a nice bar of soap is what you should wash out your mouth with. I opted for a screwdriver instead. Aunt Sylvia was staring at Scotty, obviously fascinated.

"You haven't been to bed?"

"That depends," Scotty muttered. Then he got a far-off look in his eye, and said to nobody in particular: "Have you ever spent thirty-six hours being chased by a geriatric sex fiend?"

I drained my screwdriver.

"Have a little Danish," Aunt Sylvia commanded. Scotty reached for the plate and stuck his fingers in some raspberry jelly. He stared at them in disgust, then looked beseechingly in my direction.

"You don't happen to have any eggs Benedict lying around the place, do you?"

I shook my head.

He licked the jam off his fingers, and staggered toward the vodka bottle. The drink seemed to help: he straightened himself up, then caught a glimpse of himself in the mirror over the bar. "Jesus, I forgot to shave!"

Now it was Uncle Hymie's turn to suggest that maybe the airport would be a good place for us to go, but Aunt Sylvia wasn't having any of it.

"You had a nice weekend?" she asked Scotty, who was unfortunately too far gone to pick up on the sarcasm in her voice.

"I think I'm getting too old for all this," he said. "I mean, George wouldn't leave me alone for a second." (He's complaining? I haven't even *seen* Jimmy for twelve hours!)

"What happened?" I asked, knowing he was going to tell us anyway.

"*Well,*" he began. "Just *everybody* was up there." That meant there were about four people he knew, but they behaved badly enough for it to seem like twenty. "George wants to marry me."

I couldn't see what that had to do with *everybody* being there, but I assumed there was a connection in Scotty's mind. There was.

"Murray, you wouldn't have believed it! Tim and Ted have a house up there, and there was a party going on. Rita-Rose was there, so you can imagine what the party was like—"

"Rita-Rose?" Aunt Sylvia demanded. "Who's Rita-Rose?"

"You don't want to know," Uncle Hymie told her, which was a tactical error. Tell Aunt Sylvia she doesn't want to know something, and she'll spend the next three years worming it out of you.

"*Any*way," Scotty continued, rising above the interruption, "I did my best to behave myself, but I guess I must have had one or two too many stingers."

"Or maybe five or six," I suggested.

"Don't be picky. Anyway, from what I've been told, I may have misbehaved, just slightly."

"Don't tell me," I said, too late.

"We all decided to go hit one of the bars—I don't know which one it was, but I'm sure somebody does —and apparently I forgot to get dressed first."

"Dressed?" Aunt Sylvia asked. "I thought you were at a party. You weren't dressed at the party?"

"Well, I was when it started," Scotty said virtuously.

"Besides, clothes aren't really *de rigueur* at Tim and Ted's house."

"So why does George want to marry you?" I asked. "If I were him, I'd never want to see you again."

"Which just goes to show you the difference between you and the people who love me. George thinks I need taking care of."

"You need a keeper, is what you need."

"Well, actually, I need to be kept, but I'm beginning to suspect that isn't going to happen. George is old, but he isn't rich."

This, I figured, would give Aunt Sylvia a perfect opening for a short lecture on the virtues of settling down with a nice girl instead of an old man, either rich or poor, but I was wrong. She still hadn't gotten past Scotty's manner of dress at the party and/or the bar.

"You went to a bar with no clothes on?" she asked.

Scotty nodded glumly, and poured another drink.

Aunt Sylvia appeared to be turning things over in her mind. I figured by now, with all the new data she'd absorbed over the weekend, she'd be pretty well shell-shocked, and I was right. Instead of giving Scotty a lecture, which frankly I thought he deserved, she only shrugged.

"I thought doing things like that was illegal," was all she could think of to say.

"It was," Scotty observed. Then he passed out.

I left him where he was, and started herding Aunt Sylvia and Uncle Hymie toward the airport. Aunt Sylvia made some mutterings about the advisability of staying around for a while—Scotty was obviously going to need a lot of advice when he woke up—but Uncle Hymie and I managed to convince her that whatever happened, it really wasn't any of her business. This was an entirely new concept to her, and I was sure it didn't sink in. As things eventually turned out, I was right.

By the time I got back from the airport, Scotty had come to his senses again, and it seemed things weren't as bad as they sounded. The cops had picked him up, but Scotty had dreamed up a story about how he had been on his way home when five people jumped him, and stole his clothes. He had retreated to the bar, not wanting to make a public nuisance of himself, and claimed he was in the process of borrowing some clothes when the police arrived. Since George and a few other people (all of them dressed) had backed up his story, the cops had let him go. They probably figured it would be easier to drop the whole thing than deal with Scotty. They were probably right.

After listening to his story, and knowing Scotty, I figured he'd probably get drunk sometime that week, decide he'd found true love, and move in with George. True love would last about three weeks, then we'd go through three weeks of "Why did I do it?" and wind up renting another truck to haul Scott's sofa bed out of George's place. Someday I'm going to buy that sofa bed from Scott, just so I can throw it away.

So I occupied myself during the week with Scotty's problems. On the weekend Marv and Bill arrived from L.A.

I must say, that was a very strange weekend. Marv and Bill were staying at Jimmy's place, and they seemed to take it for granted that we were lovers until late Friday night when I went home. As I left, I could have sworn that Marv and Bill looked at each other as though they thought I was some kind of nut, but I let it pass. I was, after all, beginning to feel like some kind of nut.

Most of the weekend was spent in Jimmy's apartment, while Jimmy and Marv talked medicine, and Bill and I talked sissy. It seemed to me that Jimmy and Marvin were doing an awful lot of talking alone in the kitchen, but when I mentioned this to Bill, he didn't seem worried. Well, let me tell you, if it had been my lover's ex-lover in the kitchen with my lover, I'd have been there, too. On the other hand, I'm a neurotic Jewish faggot, and Bill isn't. (Also, my *lover* wasn't in the kitchen with his ex-lover. I only wished he was!)

Sunday evening, just before Bill and Marv left, we set things up for Mother's Day. It was decided that Jimmy would stay with them, and I'd stay with Aunt Sylvia and Uncle Hymie, so we'd have another weekend of commuting from one house to another, only this time it would be in Beverly Hills instead of San Francisco. It seemed, though, that if Jimmy was going to go with me, this was the best way to work it, and I'd come to the conclusion that having Jimmy in the same city, if not the same bed, was better than not having Jimmy at all. It was beginning to look like I was going to grow old in celibacy (which sounds like it must be somewhere in Vermont).

Then, a week before we were due to go to L.A., the shit hit the fan.

What happened was this. Jimmy got a letter from Marvin, which he showed me, and, I must say, it was strange. What Marvin did was dis-invite Jimmy. It seemed Bill had gotten cold feet about the whole thing, and turned nervous about having Jimmy in their house with Marvin. Apparently as far as Bill was concerned, it was one thing for Marv and him to stay with Jimmy, but for Jimmy to stay with them was entirely another. Well, such is the mind of a hairdresser.

Bill and Marv, however, had come up with a solution. They had taken it upon themselves to call Aunt Sylvia and find out if Jimmy could stay there. Well, what could she say? Jimmy, after all, had taken her out to dinner, given her counseling. Could she turn him down? Not likely.

I promptly cleared out the week after Mother's Day. If things went haywire, as they were very likely to go, I could stay drunk for seven days and recover from the whole mess.

I was suddenly getting very nervous. I mean, sneaking a friend into my room when I was in high school was one thing. Aunt Sylvia didn't know what was going on. But this time? Not that anything was going to be happening. Aunt Sylvia has twin beds in her guest room, and what can you do in twin beds? Actually you can do practically anything but sleep, but in this case it seemed unlikely.

It was the principle of the thing. Aunt Sylvia would be wondering what was going on, and I would be wondering what she was thinking was going on, and we'd both be thinking the worst (or best, depending on whose point of view you're looking at), and I wasn't going to be getting any sleep. Instead, I was going to be wanting Jimmy, and he was going to be lying there snoring (Did he snore? I didn't know!) while I was aging a year every hour.

I could hear the conversation the next morning:

AUNT SYLVIA: Did you boys sleep all right?
JIMMY (bright-eyed and bushy-tailed): Great!

ME (bleary-eyed and dragging my tail): What's sleep?

Those few days before we went to L.A. were one of the times when I felt that my life should have closed out of town, and I could tell Jimmy wasn't feeling any better about the situation. In fact, for a while, he almost decided not to go.

But in the end, we went.

22

It was all very strange. On Saturday Jimmy and I drove down to Beverly Hills. It doesn't take very long to get there anymore. They have this freeway, with a really gorgeous name.

Interstate 5.

Now I ask you, is that a picturesque name for a highway? But after you drive it, you can see why they named it that. There wasn't anything else to call it.

Hundreds of miles, with no turns.

Also, no scenery.

You know how sometimes you're tempted to take your eyes off the road because the countryside is so interesting? Well, on Interstate 5, the most interesting thing is the white line down the middle. Two or three lanes going both ways, and you're lucky if you ever see another car. Don't try to play the Alphabet Game on that road—you never get past *a*. They put the road through a part of the state that's never been developed before, and I could see why—there's nothing there to develop.

In Beverly Hills nothing had changed. It's like the place is in a state of suspended animation, and all they do is polish the plastic once a year.

Nothing had changed at Aunt Sylvia's, either. There the house sat, pink plaster with a horseshoe driveway, and two cars on display—a big Buick and a Ford station wagon (they use it maybe to drive Hymie to the station in the morning?). Inside, nothing had changed, either. Aunt Sylvia got her taste straight out of World War II, and hasn't budged since. Actually, it wouldn't have been so bad if Aunt Sylvia hadn't gotten her furniture out of Sloane's, but what can I tell you? All that's missing is the mezuzah on the door: Aunt Sylvia sold it to a Unitarian who wanted to hedge her bets.

Aunt Sylvia did her welcome-to-my-home-be-it-ever-so-humble number, and dragged us directly to the guest room, which used to be my room.

Shock.

The twin beds were gone.

Instead, there was only one bed, which, unless my decorator's eye had failed me, was queen-size.

"Make yourselves at home," Aunt Sylvia said. "Drinks on the patio as soon as you've unpacked." By drinks, I assumed she meant Cel-Ray tonic.

Jimmy looked at me quizzically. "Did this used to be your room?" he asked.

"When it was mine, it had twin beds. This is a new addition." (Well, there were twin beds there last time I was down!)

"Which side do you want?" Jimmy asked, looking a little worried.

Your side, I thought.

"Take your choice," I said.

So we unpacked, which took all of about two minutes, and went out to the patio. (Why do southern Californians think that you have to serve drinks on the patio when it's only sixty degrees and overcast? Or is it just Aunt Sylvia?)

We had drinks on the patio.

"So how was the trip?" Uncle Hymie asked as he shook a batch of daiquiris *(daiquiris?)* that I hoped had no honey in them.

"Lovely, if you like sagebrush," I replied.

"How's Scotty?" Aunt Sylvia wanted to know as she passed out hors d'oeuvres that were mercifully free of peanut butter and pickles.

"Drunk," I replied.

We made desultory conversation while Aunt Sylvia made us all nervous with her efforts to make us feel comfortable. At six we escaped to go over and get Bill and Marv, with whom we were having dinner—alone, that night. Sunday was going to be the two-family bash.

"She seems nervous," I said when we were safe in the car. Talk about projecting!

"She probably is," Jimmy said, doing a little projecting of his own. "After all, she's never played hostess to a couple of gay people before."

"She's had Bill and Marv over for dinner."

"But they weren't going to sleep in her house," Jimmy pointed out.

Or in the same bed, I thought, and wondered what on earth was going to happen.

It wasn't hard to spot Marv and Bill's house. It was the only one on the block with a Regency façade and cyprus bushes shaped within an inch of their lives.

Also, it was the only one with a high brick wall around the whole property.

We pushed a button set in the wall next to an iron gate, and waited. After a few minutes, a Judas window in the front door opened.

"Do you suppose they have Dobermans?" I asked Jimmy as we approached the front door, which swung open as we hit the porch.

"Welcome to Paranoid Park," Marv said. "Come on in, so I can kiss you both."

We went in, and kisses were handed out all around. The only two people who didn't kiss each other were Jimmy and I, and I was frankly beginning to think that was never going to happen.

Between them, Marv and Bill had taken a perfectly decent house in Beverly Hills, and turned it into a West Hollywood faggot epic.

"It's simple," Marvin said, making one of those all-encompassing gestures that wreck the cloisonné, "but we call it home."

"You can certainly tell who lives here," Jimmy said, noncommittally. "Why the wall?"

"We value our privacy," Bill said, trying to sound demure, which wasn't easy, considering he'd bleached his hair and was wearing false eyelashes.

"I thought maybe you were afraid of the neighbors," Jimmy suggested.

"Actually, at first we were," Marv said. "It was either put up the wall, or black out the windows, and we opted for light. Park your asses and name your poison. We have everything, so don't be shy."

"Before I get polluted, how far do I have to drive for dinner?" Jimmy asked.

Jimmy doesn't like to drive drunk, which is one of his many admirable qualities. On the other hand, he doesn't think eight drinks will make him drunk, which isn't so admirable. Of course, eight drinks don't really seem to make him drunk, so I wondered why he asked that question in the first place.

"There's a new place advertising naked waiters," Marv said. "I thought we'd try it."

"Naked waiters?" I asked. "Doesn't that get a little messy?"

"Messy?" That was Bill, getting curious.

"What happens if someone gropes one of them while he's carrying a tray of soup?"

"We'll hope that doesn't happen," Marv said.

"If you're there, it'll happen," Jimmy said.

"I've given up that sort of thing. The last time I groped a waiter, Connie Curlers here threatened to divorce me."

"And that stopped you? You must be getting old."

Marvin was outraged. "Wash your mouth out! Mature. The word is mature!"

"He's getting old," Bill said.

Marv shrugged. "So I'm getting old. Aren't we all?"

"We all aren't admitting it," I put in.

"But all you have to do is look at us," Marv said, pouring the drinks.

"Speak for yourself," Bill said. "I haven't changed at all since the day we met."

"True, but your youth washes off with cold cream every night," Marv remarked as he handed out the hooch. "Never marry a hair-burner. They start believing their own line of bullshit, and you wind up living in a branch office of Elizabeth Arden."

We all tried to make ourselves comfortable on the Louis XVI furniture, which was impossible. As I looked around the room I began getting a vision of some broken-down decorator skipping up and down

Robertson Boulevard, chortling about the doctor and the hairdresser with too much money and not enough taste. The vision was interrupted by Bill telling me that he'd done the whole thing himself.

"You didn't," I said, trying not to look stricken. "You certainly are a man of many talents." I didn't add that decorating was not one of them. Fortunately, Jimmy jumped into the conversation and asked how living in Beverly Hills was.

"Not so bad," Marv said. "At first I wasn't sure we'd be allowed north of Sunset (eat your heart out, Aunt Sylvia!), but actually the neighbors don't seem to mind a bit. I think they were afraid we were going to molest their children at first, but when they found out we weren't, they all started getting friendly. Now it's at the point where all the women want Bill's recipes, and the men want to know how to make their lawns look like ours."

"But, my God," I said. "There isn't another faggot for three miles!" To me, this was like being in Purgatory!

"Who needs faggots?" Marv said. "We spend most of our time right here, and we have lots of straight friends. Now and then we go over to see friends in West Hollywood, but for us, this is fine. We don't bother the natives, and they don't bother us. And you'd be surprised how peaceful things can be when you're not surrounded by gay people all the time."

"But don't you get lonely?" (Me again.)

"We have each other."

I was starting to hate them. How dare they sit there and tell us they were happy? Everybody knows that gay people are miserable, right?

[176]

We finished up our drinks and adjourned to Hollywood and the restaurant.

The waiters, as advertised, were naked.

The clientele seemed to be made up of rejects from a very dark steambath.

We got a table and ordered drinks.

There's something, I have to admit, about being served a drink by a waiter whose cock is waving in your face that makes you lose both your thirst and your appetite. We did our duty and rubbernecked the waiters. Finally Jimmy spoke.

"If what I've seen so far is representational of the meat they serve here, I suggest we go elsewhere." Strangely, nobody disagreed with him.

We wound up on Beverly Boulevard at a Mexican restaurant that you could call mixed—the clientele is ninety percent gay and the staff is ninety percent straight. Leave it to the gay crowd to find the restaurants that serve good drinks and good food at good prices.

From there we proceeded to a place on La Cienega that had undergone a sea change. It had started out as a Polynesian epic restaurant, and converted at some point into a disco, with the booths replaced by light units, and the bars pumping beer instead of mai tais. All in all, something of an improvement, particularly for those of us who prefer the Bee Gees to Don Ho. Things were beginning to look up. The drinks were good, and I decided I might as well have several of them so that I'd be able to get some sleep that night.

At two, we headed back to Beverly Hills.

By the time we got back to Aunt Sylvia's, everybody had gone to bed, so I suggested we have a nightcap. Jimmy didn't feel like it. I didn't either, really, but one has to do something to avoid the unavoidable, doesn't one?

So we adjourned to the bedroom, and I immediately headed for the bathroom to brush my teeth. By the time I got back, Jimmy was in a robe, and *he* headed for the bathroom.

I undressed, and slid into bed, staying as close to the edge as possible and hiding my head in the pillow. Also, I kept the covers clutched provocatively around my neck.

A few minutes later Jimmy came in, snapped off the lights, and I could feel the bed move as he climbed into his side.

For a long time there was a silence as we both clung precariously to the edges of the bed. I finally decided it was ridiculous. If Jimmy was going to stay all the way over on his edge, I could at least relax.

So I rolled over on my back, and as I did, I felt his hand close on mine.

"Murray?" he said in a sort of strangled voice.

"Hmmm?"

"Do you mind if I kiss you good-night?"

Mind? Me mind? What was he, some kind of nut? So I rolled over, and his arms folded around me.

All of a sudden all the tension went out of my body, and I realized I was home.

I mean, I was really home.

Then he kissed me. The kiss lasted all night, and the last thing I remember is that it was starting to get light when I fell asleep with my head on his chest and his arms still around me.

The dialogue at breakfast went something like this:

AUNT SYLVIA: Did you boys sleep all right?

JIMMY & ME (staring bovinely into each other's eyes): Sleep? What's sleep?

AUNT SYLVIA: So, have some more lox!

I don't remember much about the rest of the weekend. I guess we all went out to dinner, but I haven't any idea where, or what, if anything, was said.

Sunday night was even better than Saturday night, because we didn't go anywhere but to bed.

Monday we left, and instead of driving back up Interstate 5, we decided to go up the coast and stop at Monterey for a few days.

Tuesday, we said the hell with Monterey, and went home.

Wednesday, I started packing. (Did I mention earlier that I liked Jimmy's place better than my own?)

Thursday, I dropped Linda Goldberg a note, suggesting that if she's still hunting for a man, she should try going to a psychiatrist. If it worked for me, why shouldn't it work for her?

Friday, I wrote to Aunt Sylvia.

23

Dear Aunt Sylvia,

News! By the time you get this, I will have moved. I don't know exactly how it all happened, but I'm moving into Jimmy Coleman's apartment. I won't have to change anything there, of course, since I designed the whole thing myself, and I won't have to take much except my clothes, since I made sure he was fully equipped when I redid him. The only question now is what to do with this place. For the moment, I'm turning it over to Scott, and charging him a disgusting amount of rent. (How often can you find a furnished house that's furnished with Waterford crystal?)

It all happened at your house. God bless you for replacing those twin beds. It seems that Jimmy was just as worried about me as I was about him. He'd been wanting to make a pass at me, but was afraid I wasn't interested. So when it happened that, through no fault of our own, we were in the same bed together, Nature took her glorious course, and I'm pleased to report that our compatibility in bed is just as good as our compatibility out of bed.

You may have noticed something going on between us on Sunday. I wouldn't know, because I wasn't noticing anything on Sunday.

Anyway, you're going to have to come up here again. Jimmy and I have decided to throw a big party three weeks from Saturday to celebrate our finally putting it all together, and to serve notice on our various and sundry friends that neither one of us is single anymore.

That, of course, is when we'll find out who our friends are: the ones who were only interested in us because we were single won't come. (Wouldn't it be a riot if nobody came at all? Not that we'd care particularly, and it would save a lot on booze.)

Marv and Bill will be up that weekend, staying at my house with Scott. (If they didn't want Jimmy staying with them, I don't want them staying with us!) So you'll know them and Scott, and of course Uncle Hymie will know a lot of the other people from when he was up here a few weeks ago. Also, we're inviting Sam Levitz and his friend. He's not much like Miriam, Aunt Sylvia, but he's very nice.

I'm not inviting Rita-Rose, so there's a good chance the party won't be raided.

Needless to say, we both had a wonderful time

down there. Thanks so much for putting us up. Your hospitality was more than I could ever have asked for.

Love from both of us,
Murray

P.S. So now you're one up on Rachel Pomerantz —*her* son only married a hairdresser!—M.R.

Naturally, Aunt Sylvia had the last word.

Dear Murray,

I think I'm going to have to write to Jimmy and tell him he's married a not-so-smart decorator. On the other hand, you have apparently married a not-so-smart psychiatrist. Of course, I don't suppose either one of you has settled down enough yet to figure things out, so I will set you straight (you should pardon the word).

Don't be so hard on Marvin and Bill. They were perfectly willing to put Jimmy up.

But I got to thinking.

Sylvia, I said to myself. If Jimmy Coleman is at Bill and Marvin's, and Murray is here, what can possibly happen?

So I asked Marvin what he knew about how Jimmy was feeling, and he told me when he and Bill were up there, he spent all his time in the kitchen listening to Jimmy crying the blues about how he was afraid you weren't interested in him. It turned out he was feeling the same way about you that you were feeling about him. (You thought you told me something I didn't already know? Hah! Everybody knows that Jewish mothers know everything, even if they are only aunts.)

So then I got to thinking some more.

Sylvia, I said to myself. What would happen if you had Hymie move the twin beds out of the guest room and you put in one big bed instead? But not too big. (What I got, they call a queen-size bed. Funny? I thought so!)

So that's what I did, and then Marvin and Bill and Hymie and I figured out that story of why Jimmy couldn't stay with them. After all, if the story hadn't sounded good, you'd have smelled a rat.

Then we all sat back and waited for nature to take its course.

Four times Marvin and Bill called here on Sunday morning to find out what happened. When you two still weren't up by ten thirty, we all knew what happened.

Right? Of course, right.

As to the housing arrangements when we come up for the party. I think you ought to have Marv and Bill stay with you two, and Hymie and I will stay at your house with Scott. For one thing, I already know the layout of that place, and where things are.

For another thing, if I'm staying with you, I'll feel like I have to help you clean up the mess after the party. Frankly, Murray, I think I've done enough for you two, and you can clean up your own mess!

Also, from what I know of your friend Scotty, he

could use a good Jewish mother. Now that I've got you all straightened out (you should pardon the expression), I think I might as well start on him.

Mazel Tov.

Love,
Aunt Sylvia

P.S. Hymie and I have sent the queen-size bed to you and Jimmy. One thing every marriage needs is a bed that belongs to the two of you. Then neither one of you has to worry about who might have been there before him. Besides, who ever heard of a guest room without twin beds? —A.S.